THE
CONTRACTOR

BY

DAVID SCOTT MEYERS

WITH ILLUSTRATIONS BY

HANNAH NICOLE MEYERS

The Contractor

Copyright © 2018 by David Scott Meyers

Published by Fin Scott Publishing
http://finscottpublishing.weebly.com

Cover design by:
Fin Scott Publishing
Cover art by:
Hannah Nicole Meyers

ISBN-13: 978-1-7320320-0-2

To my beloved wife, Samantha,

my loving children, Hannah, Robert, and Ava,

my brothers, Bob and Jeff,

my parents, Bob and Eileen,

and all my ancestors that have come before me...

Back in 2009, my brother, Jeff, came to me with an idea for a script. He knew that I had written another screenplay that the film production company of one of my best friend's had already completed filming and was in post-production. The handwritten sheet of notes that he gave me would be the foundation of what would become this book, The Contractor. I read through the notes, excited that my brother was showing interest in one of my passions and sharing his ideas with me, with the hopes that I could take his idea and make it into a film. I saw great potential in the plot, and I saw how I could take what he had given me and turn it into something that had my signature on it as well. The more and more I wrote, the keys on the laptop just flowed. I am so glad that Jeff trusted me with such a task.

Over the last 16 years, I have been obsessed with researching my family's history, as well as my wife's. Between the two branches, I have connected well over 17,000 people. My wife's paternal grandfather's ancestry stems from both Western and Southern Tennessee. I used my research on this branch to influence the characters and setting of The Contractor. Although Fellowship is strictly a fictional town, its location and some of the characteristics of the area are based on geographically-accurate details, ideals, and terminology. Almost all of the characters in this novel are named after genuine family members from my wife's side of the family, although the names were mixed up, so not one character was identifiable with actual people, living or dead. The family names of the people are easily tied to the region in which Fellowship is situated. The town of Fellowship was named from a local cemetery in the area where a lot of my wife's family are buried. I did this to authenticate and validate the story and to share with you, the reader, an emotional and visual attachment of the tangible feel that you would get if you ever traveled to this area. I have been to the area several times now, and the first time I wasn't sure what to think. I was so nervous to enter this realm that my wife called home and meet the extended family that she had grown up with. I can honestly say from the very first time that the laid-back, welcoming, open-arm hugs that I received that first summer touched my soul, and I want to share that feeling with you. I still feel that way every time we go back. You should know AND feel that if you were to ever travel to this part of the country, you would get the same warmth and love that I received.

I plan on making this venture into Fellowship a 3-part series, and I have already begun working on the second book, _The Sheriff_. The books will all be connected with developing details throughout each novel. You may not get the whole story with each book, but by the end of the 3rd installment, you should have answers to it all, and you will know and love OR hate each and every character. I hope that you will continue on this journey with me through a *culture so universal, yet so unique. And I can't wait to share my story with you...*

David Scott Meyers

Acknowledgements:

Thanks to my family and close friends who have always shown support in my love for writing.

Special Thanks to my brother, Jeff, who gave me the basic concept for the plot of this book. Sorry I changed it up a little, but it was a great storyline. I wouldn't have this book without it. I am so honored that he had the confidence in me and trusted me with his story.

Special Thanks to my daughter, Hannah, for lending her amazing talent to illustrating this novel. I definitely couldn't have done a better job. Everything that I described, she got down with a little graphite and whole lot of eraser. Her work was definitely a strive for perfection, and I couldn't have asked for anything more than what she gave. I love sharing my passion with you, and it shows in the brilliance you have given back to me. I am ecstatic to have the opportunity to work with you, and I can't wait to collaborate in the future. You definitely have prospective potential. Love you, Hannah.

Extra Special Thanks to my loving wife, Samantha, for never giving up on me, and when I was feeling lost and blocked, she held strong with her faith and pushed me to keep going. I love you for many reasons, but I cannot thank you enough for believing in me and being honest about my passion. When I doubted myself, you stood your ground and kept me from sinking in the sand of my own uncertainty. Your dedication is inspiring to us all. I love you.

CHAPTER 1

A blue sedan with government plates drove down the long stretch of two-lane highway. Finally coming across the only driveway for miles, it turned in and pulled alongside a farmhouse. Turning off the car and stepping out the door was a tall gentleman in a relaxed, black suit and a fedora. Tennessee in mid-July was a little hot for a suit, but it was required in his profession, so it was bearable. The man closed the car door and approached the front steps of the house. As he climbed the steps, he noticed a sign on the door. It read: FRIENDS – GO 'ROUND BACK, PEDDLERS – GO 'ROUND SOMEWHERE ELSE.

The man didn't attempt to knock on the front door. He walked around to the back steps of the house and knocked on the back door. "Just a minute!" grumbled a loud, male voice from within.

The man in the suit took one step back and waited. Three minutes passed before an elderly man stepped through the open, main door and pushed open the screen door. The old man squinted through the steam on his glasses.

"Do I know you? You don't look familiar."

The man in the suit replied, "No, sir, you don't. My name is Elbert London."

"What can I do for you, Mr... uh...?"

1

"London."

"Right. Right. What can I do for you, Mr. London?"

Elbert London smiled and held a clipboard up to his own face. Flipping over two pages, he read for a moment and then looked up at the old man.

"Are you a Mr. Elias Morgan?"

The old man smiled, "Yes, sir. I am a Elias Morgan."

"Elias <u>Jedidiah</u> Morgan?"

"Well, you appear to know who I am, so why don't you tell me what this is about."

"Sir, I am Elbert London, and I…"

"We've established that," Elias interrupted.

Mr. London continued, "…and I am with the Tennessee State Highway Commission."

"Well, I am Elias Jedidiah Morgan, and I am with the Ridgeway Farms of Ridgeway Crossing Commission," he said smugly.

"So this is Ridgeway Farms?" He checked his clipboard. "I'm in the right place, then."

"No, Mr. London. You're in the wrong place."

"I don't understand." Elbert London took a step back off the porch.

"I'm gonna explain this to you with the utmost respect. I know why you're here. I know that this is nothing personal. It's just your job. I know that you wanna plow through my ancestral ground and slap an ugly, new interstate right in the middle of Ridgeway Crossing. I know that it started twenty years ago, then fifteen, then ten, then five, and now you're here. It's never the same person, but it's always the same thing. And every time, I tell you no. What makes today any different?"

"Mr. Morgan. May I call you Elias?"

"Mr. Morgan will do just fine," Elias snapped back.

"Mr. Morgan. Do you realize what this interstate would do for the fine state of Tennessee? It would provide a quicker route for transporting people and goods. It would bring much-needed federal government funding to programs for our state. It would benefit many people in many ways."

"Do you, Mr. London, realize what that damn road would do for me? It would provide me with unwanted traffic traveling through my protected homeland. It would bring noise from cars, pollution from exhaust, garbage from inconsiderate motorists, and continuous construction that would go on forever. This area doesn't need growth, commerce, or technology. Your interstate would destroy this natural section of what my family has slaved over for the last two hundred years."

"Two hundred years? Don't you think it's about time that you give a little piece of this land back to the people? The highway commission doesn't want all of it.

You got what?" Elbert London looked at his clipboard. "Over a hundred acres here? Just a fraction of that..."

"Just a fraction of that is too much!" Elias yelled. "Every time that I tell one of you guys that I'm never selling any land, you just jot down some notes and leave. Sooner or later though, someone comes back.

Elbert was getting angry. "You know, Mr. Morgan that the government can just come in, take whatever land it wants away from you, and give you whatever they want to pay for it?"

Elias smiled. "It's been twenty years since my first visitor from your commission and no one's taken it yet. I'd like to see them try. Idle threats just make me feel that much more secure."

Elbert London looked once again at his clipboard, flipping through sheets of paper. He noticed something that he hadn't before. "It says here on my paperwork that you have no living descendants or kin of any kind. You can't live forever, Mr. Morgan. Everyone's gotta die sometime. The commission can just bide its time and wait to probate the estate. Sooner or later... " He shook his clipboard at Elias. "...sooner or later."

"My estate is well taken care of. You're going to be waitin' a long time, sir. There won't be a probate. This land will be government-free forever." Elias displayed a big, toothy grin.

"I don't see how... " Elbert stated.

4

"What you need to be seein' is your rear windshield as you're backin' that car out of my driveway. I've obliged your persistence long enough. You've been trespassing for twenty minutes now. I suggest you get in your car and go try to peddle that road on the other side of Fellowship, 'cause it ain't goin' in here. Besides, can't you read the sign on my front door?" Elias slammed the screen door, then the kitchen door.

Elbert London got back into his blue sedan, backed out of the driveway, and pulled away from Ridgeway Farms, shaking his head in disbelief.

CHAPTER 2

A week had passed since Elias's visit from the Highway Commission, and life was once again back to normal for Elias. The sweltering heat outside was unbearable. The perennial flowers by Ellen's garden next to the woodshed were slouched over like a town drunk. Even with no one willing to care for his wife's flowers, they were still surviving somehow. The sun beat down with no clouds for miles. Tempting as it was to go out back and sit under the willow tree for some afternoon shade, the effort to step outside was not worth the result. The number of elderly deaths rises in times like these. Even though Elias wanted to go spend time with Ellen, he wasn't going to take the chance of leaving the house today. There never had been central air installed, and the oscillating fan wouldn't oscillate. Heck, nowadays it didn't even want to run. Elias sat there in the dark, looking out the window. It was better in the dark: less electricity, less heat. The battery in his portable radio went out last week. The milk in the fridge had spoiled two days ago. There he sat. He couldn't remember the last time he had changed clothes. Who was he going to impress?

He stared out that window long enough for the "square" sun shining in on his west bedroom wall to go from the ceiling to the floor and then across the floor until it disappeared midday. By then, the temperature would come down a few degrees, enough to get up out of bed and make it into the kitchen. Then, Elias would scrape enough mold off the loaf of bread to spread some homemade preserves on a slice for lunch. He never had a television in the house. There was never any noise. Sometimes, the house would settle or the wind would rattle some windows, but other than that, it was quiet . . .

It had been that way since Ellen had passed. She was the lifeblood of that farm. She would tend to her garden, go into town for church meetings, and spend hours talking to Elias. She would talk and he would mostly just listen. But now that she was gone, life stood still. Most days, the clock hands would be the only thing moving on the farm. Elias could still hear Ellen's voice though. Every gentle breeze had the tone of her voice, whispering confessions of her love for him. He would wake up some mornings and smell a bold, distinct scent of Ellen's freshly fried eggs and brewed coffee. He would scoot as fast as he could to the kitchen to find nothing but a stack of dishes in the sink. He would sit at the kitchen table and sob waterless tears.

Ellen had passed only six months ago, but to Elias, it seemed like years. The time just dragged with no laughter to fill the void. Once a day, Elias would travel out to the back end of his 100-acre property to visit

Ellen. You see, way back in the corner of the lot, there was a family cemetery. It was back in the woods, surrounded by a shrub fence to hide it from most people. He didn't get any visitors ever, so he would spend a big portion of the day, sitting on an old wooden bench, talking to Ellen. He would reminisce about the good ol' days. Some of his ramblings were happy and some were sad, but just to be able to talk to someone, even if they didn't reply, made Elias content. He could vent and not have anyone argue back. Besides, it was Ellen that he was talking to, and she would surely understand his thoughts anyway. In life and in death, they were connected in a way that no other person could ever reach with either of them. He would bring a lunch with him sometimes and stay there until sunset, so they could enjoy it together.

Today, however, he did not go to see Ellen. It was so hot that he couldn't possibly stand sitting on that old bench for a whole day. Ellen would understand. After he finished his lunch, he stood by the back porch window, staring out at that old rickety barn just beyond the driveway. He stared at it for at least an hour before any sort of distracting thought hit him. Then, he pulled away from the lace curtains that Ellen had made and slapped on his old boots with a new determination. Sure, the heat was bad today, but why should that stop him? "Don't think about it. Keep moving," he thought out loud.

He pushed out through the back door, and the heat slapped him like an invisible wall. He had been having trouble walking lately, so it was more of a shuffle-step than a march. He made his way over to the other side of the driveway where his old beat-up car sat, decaying more every day.

He opened the creaking driver's side door. The rusty smell of dust particles filled his nose as the door opened fully. He coughed as he sat down on the dusty bench seat, causing another cloud to emerge. Coughing some more, he put the key in the ignition and turned over the engine. It had been down for a while, so it took some time before it would fire up and warm to a decent running condition.

Elias sat there with the door open and his left leg sticking out of it until the car was good and ready. The car, like his house had no air conditioning in it, and steam rose from the hood. The car was so hot inside that Elias's vision was blurry. Once the car was idling smooth, Elias grabbed his left thigh and slowly pulled his leg inside the car, shutting the door behind him. He rolled the windows down, so he wouldn't pass out, and started to back down the driveway. He stopped after a few feet, shifted to drive and pulled forward while turning, so he could execute a three-point turn. It was much easier to drive this worn-down car forward than it was to reverse it. The car rode like Elias walked. The engine would rev and then idle...rev and then idle. Elias had to keep constant pressure on the gas pedal just to keep the car from dying. He got to the end of the gravel driveway and looked both ways for traffic. Of course, there wasn't any. Regardless of the heat today, no one ever came out this way anymore . . . for anything. He turned right onto the paved two-lane highway heading into town.

CHAPTER 3

It was nine miles down this paved road into town. Elias took it slow and easy on his car. The heat was now slowly starting to die down in the mid-afternoon. It took him about 35 to 40 minutes to reach the outskirts of town. He drove down the main drag and pulled in towards the grocery store. He got out of the car and hobbled into the store. He only went in for a few staples like bread, milk, butter, lunchmeat, eggs, cereal, coffee, and bacon. He made his way around the store, filling the basket that he was carrying. He slowly made his way to the checkout.

The cashier, Florence Pope, was surprised to see him. She spoke. "Haven't seen you in about a month, Elias. How are you holding up?"

Elias never answered. He paid the lady and snatched his grocery bag from the end of the conveyor belt.

"Stubborn, old coot," the cashier mumbled as he shuffled out the automatic doors.

After the grocery store, he drove over to the gas station and asked the attendant, Bobby Willis, to fill up his tank. It didn't take long because he hadn't driven the car in a long time, and there was still at least a half a tank left in it.

"Mornin', Elias. This car looks like it could use an oil change. How 'bout it?" Bobby asked.

Elias mumbled at him, "I ain't drivin' it to Utah." He paid Bobby for the gas and drove off.

Finally, he drove over to the hardware store. This was his whole purpose for going outside and heading to town today. All morning long, he kept staring at that weather-beaten, old barn. He had been putting off so many jobs around the farm, partially because of his health and age, but mostly out of sadness and loneliness. He had been depressed for so long, and it was wearing him down. After wasting most of the morning, Elias's thoughts finally collected, and he sprung to action . . . well, the best that he could.

He kept thinking to himself, "What am I doing to myself? I've wasted six months of my already mostly-spent life. I cannot keep going on like this. Ellen wouldn't want me to sit around, wallowing in my self-pity. She would want me to remember her fondly as I went on with my life. I can't spend any more time sitting around, waiting to die. I might as well do something. That way, even if I still die soon, I can't say that I wasn't trying to live."

As Elias shuffled into the hardware store, he was thinking of the items he needed for his first project, the barn. He wasn't going to try to repair the walls or tear it down and build a new one. He just wanted to reinforce the walls to keep them from falling over. The northwest area of Tennessee that Elias lived in was known for tornadoes and high winds during a storm, and although he himself had never experienced one, he sure wanted to be prepared for it, if it ever did come his way. The house that he and Ellen lived in was his parents' home, and it was built sturdy and sound. The barn, however, was original to the land. It was built by his great, great, great grandfather, who was a founding member of the county and the original settler of this land. It still stood today, but it was in horrible shape. He could not bear to tear it down, out of respect for his founding ancestors. He did not want to wreck any of his valuable farming equipment inside the barn, either.

Elias decided to preserve the building in the best way he knew how. He was going to leave the structure alone, but his plan was to build a solid, cinder-block wall to reinforce the inside perimeter of the barn. It would stand about 10' tall and it would be spaced about 2' away from the original walls. The barn itself would sway with a strong breeze, and Elias took that into consideration when drafting his design. He just wanted to brace the barn if it swayed too much.

Now, he needed materials to build his cinder-block wall. As he entered the store, Elias noticed a truck parked in the lot. This was a fairly new truck, and he hadn't had a new vehicle in a long time. He stood there for a moment admiring it and noticing the lettering on the driver's side door. The words INDEPENDENT CONTRACTOR stood out bold in Elias's mind. He continued on into the store to look for his materials, still thinking about that truck. He thought to himself, "All it needs is a new paint job."

Once inside the store, Elias searched for mortar mix and new trowels. He was going to need some drop cloths, a new shovel, and a new wheelbarrow. The wheelbarrow on the farm now belonged to Elias's grandfather, and the wooden handle has all but rotted away. Elias kept thinking to himself how helpful it would be to have a truck to haul all of these materials back home. He was going to have to stop at the landscaping place down the road in Forrester Grove as well to get the cinder-block ordered. "How am I going to get that home?" he mumbled out loud.

And then, a thought just flowed through his head. "The truck! Why don't I go outside and ask that contractor for the use of his truck to help me get this stuff home? Better yet. Why don't I pay him to do the job for me? That way, I still get the job done, I'm satisfied with the work, and I don't have to sweat myself to death." A smile came across Elias's face. "That's perfect", he said.

Elias left the cart full of the items he needed right where he stood, and he limped quickly out the door, looking for the owner of the truck. By chance and good timing, the contractor was just arriving at his truck and loading tools into the truck bed. Elias hobbled over to the truck and paused, putting his hands on his knees and hunching over to catch up with some deep breaths. The contractor noticed Elias and stopped what he was doing to tend to him.

"Can I help you, sir?" the contractor asked.

Elias removed one hand from his knee and lifted one finger as if to say "Hold on a minute while I catch my breath". He looked up at the contractor while still hunched over and without having to say a word, the contractor nodded in acknowledgement. The contractor stood there waiting for Elias for a few moments. As Elias caught his breath, he stood up, wearily.

"Are you all right?"

Elias nodded, looking at him and spoke, "I'm sorry to startle you. The name's Elias Morgan. On my way in the store, I noticed that your truck said that you're an independent contractor."

"That's right", the contractor answered.

"You have to forgive me, I'm old. My thoughts don't always arrive at the right time. I didn't put the pieces together until I was halfway through the store. Once I realized what I had just walked past, I ran out the door to catch you before you left."

"What did you walk past?" Elias had peaked the contractor's interest.

"An opportunity", Elias replied. "I live on a farm, nine miles out of town. I am currently working on a project to stabilize my barn. I am at that age where I can no longer work as I once did. You, as a contractor, can help me complete my job, if you're available and interested."

"I am interested. I can always use the extra work."

"Besides", Elias chuckled. "You have a truck."

"What does that have to do with anything?" the contractor inquired.

"I have no way to bring the stuff home with me. Part of the job requires you hauling the material from the landscaping place in Forrester Grove to my farm. And... I like trucks, too", Elias mumbled the last part under his breath.

"That won't be a problem. What exactly do you need?" he asked Elias.

"Let's go back inside the store, and I can tell you what exactly it is that I want done. You are a better judge than me of what tools and materials you'll need to get the job done. Sound good?"

"I was just on my way home from work today", the contractor replied exhaustedly. "But sure, let's go."

Elias and the contractor turned and headed back inside the hardware store to go over design plans. As they entered the door, Elias looked back over his shoulder at the truck. "Nice . . . very nice", he mumbled to himself.

CHAPTER 4

The next morning, Elias was up and out of bed early. He wanted to get a head start on the details of the barn. He took a fast shower, got dressed, went downstairs, and fixed himself a bowl of cereal and some fresh coffee. He hurried through breakfast and scurried, not shuffled but scurried, through the door on the back porch, heading towards the barn. The contractor had followed him home last night, and he dropped off most of the tools and materials that they would need. He was supposed to stop off at the landscaping place over in Forrester Grove to get the cinder-block this morning before coming out to Elias's place again. The contractor wouldn't be able to haul it all in one day, but there was no rush on the job. Elias told him to take his time, but deep down Elias's heart skipped with anticipation.

Elias went out to the barn and started moving some hay away from the wall where they were going to start. Once the hay was out of the way, he swept that whole area. He laid out some drop cloths on the floor nearby where the foundation of the new wall would sit. He grabbed the trowels and the shovel and laid them out near the drop cloth. The mortar mix was ready in the barn alongside the wheelbarrow. The last thing he had to do was drag the hose to the barn from the house for mixing the concrete.

By the time he finished all of his preparation, it was time for lunch and the contractor was just arriving. The contractor pulled down the long driveway and parked near the barn. Elias heard him coming up the driveway and stepped out of the barn to greet him.

He approached the truck as the contractor exited the vehicle.

"Good morning, Elias."

"Been waitin' on ya all morning. It's afternoon now."

"Sorry. I got hung up at the landscaping place in Forrester Grove. Ran into an old associate. We exchanged unpleasantries for a few minutes, and then I picked up a load of cinder-block and headed out here."

"Don't you mean pleasantries?"

"Nope. Long story."

"Well, let's get started," Elias said. "Or should I start making supper now?"

"No. We'll get started. You open the barn door, and I'll back the truck in so I can start unloading the block."

"All right."

Elias shuffled over to the barn door while the contractor got back in the truck. He turned the truck around and backed it in through the barn doors until

Elias held up his hand to stop. He put it in park and shut off the engine, emerging from the cab. Elias began heading over to the tailgate to drop it down. The contractor raced over to the tailgate and held his hand in front of Elias.

"Never mind that. You don't need to be unloading blocks in your condition. Let me handle that. I'm in much better shape to handle a job like that. Besides, what are you paying me for?"

Elias answered back in a snarling voice, "I'll have you know that when I was but a ripe, old age of 14, I was plowing that field out beyond the wood shed with no horse pulling it. I've handled many a job that most people wouldn't dream of being capable of doing. You think that just because I'm in my seventies that I can't tackle a simple job like unloading a truck bed?"

"I'm sorry, sir. I didn't mean any insult by my comments. I just thought that you've probably spent your whole life doing work such as this, and that you may not have wanted to help me with it. I figured that you didn't want to waste your time, and that may have been the reason why you were paying me to do the job."

"I'm no backwoods hillbilly. I know what you meant by the words you used and the context you used them in. I can handle helping you out, but if you insist on doing it all yourself . . . then, be my guest."

21

Elias shuffled back away from the tailgate, and the contractor stepped in to start removing blocks.

"Based on your dimensions, Elias, I'm going to have to make several trips back to the landscaping supply store."

"I'm not in any hurry to get the job done. You don't have to make more than one trip a day. Stop off and pick up a load on your way out here each morning. You can work until the supply is gone and then leave for the day when you're done. Do the same each day and we'll have this support wall up in no time."

"Sounds good to me. I haven't had a lot of jobs lately, so I can take my time with this job and make sure it's perfect."

"Since you got such a late start today, don't worry about putting any of the wall together. Just unload the blocks and get everything ready for tomorrow. Bring another load in the morning and we'll be a day ahead on block supply."

"Great!"

The contractor hadn't had a good night's sleep the night before anyway. This would give him a chance to get home early and rest up for tomorrow. He didn't expect Elias to be such a lenient boss. He assumed that Elias was going to be demanding, nosy and in the way. This is probably going to be the easiest job that the contractor ever had. If only more people were like this, then his job wouldn't be as cumbersome as it usually is. He began unloading the truck bed with a large grin on his face. Elias pointed out exactly where to start stacking them, and he turned to the contractor and spoke.

"There's no point in me standing here watching you unload this truck in the heat. I'm going to go inside the house for some shade. Just close the barn door and latch it with the wood when you're done. I'll see you in the morning."

The contractor stopped to look at Elias and acknowledge him, "Thanks, boss. See you in the morning."

Elias turned back towards the door and began shuffling out towards the house. The contractor noticed Elias caressing the curves of the truck as he made his way out of the barn.

"Old man really loves his trucks, I guess."

The contractor resumed stacking the blocks until he was done. He closed the bed of the truck and pulled the truck outside. Then, he got out and closed and latched the barn door behind him. As he got back in the truck, he looked up at the farmhouse and noticed a curtain from the kitchen window move. Not thinking anything of it, the contractor shrugged his shoulders and pulled down the driveway to the road. He turned out onto the road and headed back to town. "Time to get some rest," he thought.

The next morning, the contractor arrived at Elias's farm at the same time that Elias was leaving the back door. Elias had a smile on his face as he unbarred the barn door and opened it for the contractor. The contractor backed his truck in again with a full load of cinder block. He exited the cab as Elias approached the driver's side door.

"Morning, Elias."

"Ready to get started today?"

"Yes, sir. I got a good night's sleep last night, and I have more than enough energy to tackle the day."

"Good. Good. You should get an excellent head start since you arrived so promptly this morning."

Elias turned to head back into the house. He seemed a little sad about going in, and the contractor noticed his change in demeanor.

"You know, if you would like to stay out here in the barn with me and keep me company, you won't be in my way at all. I would actually like the conversation. It helps to keep the day moving. I'm sure that you're day probably drags as well."

Elias's face changed and a smile grew where loneliness had once been.

"I'd appreciate that. Don't get many visitors out here, and the days get longer and longer as I get older."

"We should probably start by digging a trench the dimensions of the first wall, so I can set up a frame to pour the foundation. Then, I can start putting the first layer of block down and pour the foundation in around it. That should help to make a sturdier wall."

"Sounds good." Elias was just happy to have someone here to help him with this job. He realized now that this was his only option. He never would have been able to do this on his own. He smiled to himself, knowing he made the right call.

Elias had already marked off the area to start the first wall, so the contractor was able to just start digging. He took into account for the wooden frame and expanded the trench's overall square footage. The contractor started digging. By 10:30, he had finished the trench down the first wall, at least eighteen inches deep. Rather than continuing to dig, he stopped at the end of the first wall and started to lay out the frame.

"Good thinking," said Elias. "We'll just take this one wall at a time. I want each wall to be independent of each other and seal off at the ends to add support to the edges of the original barn wall."

The contractor questioned, "Are you sure that's how you want it? The wall would be sturdier if it was all one piece."

"That's understandable, but I don't need to just have an inner, sturdy wall. I'm trying to preserve the outer barn at the same time as protecting my equipment inside. I want support if the barn sways, not a whole new inner barn."

"O.K. You're the paying customer. You know what you want, and I'll make it to your specifications."

"Thank you for not arguing. It would be pointless because I would just end up getting my way anyway."

Now that the first trench was done, the contractor set down the first layer of cinder block.

"Are you getting hungry?" Elias asked.

"Actually, yeah." The contractor's stomach grumbled aloud. "I just ate a small breakfast, so I could get out of the house early and get a jumpstart."

Elias stood up. "I'll go in the house while you're laying down the first layer, and I'll make us some lunch. How's that sound?"

"Sounds good. We should be done about the same time."

Elias left the barn and headed in towards the house. The contractor kept plugging away at setting the first layer down in the trench, making sure that the spacing was correct and that the entire layer was level. As he worked, he thought to himself about how nice Elias was being about the whole job. "Imagine... two perfect strangers, generations apart, getting along working on a job together like old friends."

As he finished up double-checking the spacing, he heard the back door to the house slam shut. Elias had just emerged with a tray with some sandwiches on it and two cans of soda. He shuffled into the barn where the contractor still knelt down by his immediate work.

"Perfect timing," the contractor stated. "How am I doing boss?"

"Looks good," said Elias. "Why don't you come over here and have a sandwich?"

The contractor stood up and followed Elias over to some hay bales that were set up like a table and chairs.

As they sat down on the hay, Elias handed the contractor a sandwich. "I hope you don't mind turkey. I only picked up a few items at the market the last time."

"Turkey's fine," said the contractor, practically snatching the sandwich from Elias and shoving half of it into his mouth.

Elias smiled, "Hard work'll do that to you."

As Elias took interest in the sandwich before him, the contractor kept watching Elias. He was curious about the old man, all alone on this farm.

"Elias?" he asked.

"Huh?" Elias looked up from his sandwich with half a piece of crust hanging from the corner of his mouth.

"Tell me about yourself."

"What do you mean? What do you want to know?"

"Whatever you want to tell me. Start from the beginning, if you want. This is going to be a long job with just the two of us. We might as well get acquainted, if I'm going to be spending a lot of time here."

"Sure, I guess," Elias said.

"Have you always lived on this farm?"

"Oh, you want the beginning." Elias's face lit up... as it always did when he was able to share his family's journey with anyone that seemed interested. "Well, my family came over from England and settled in Virginia in the 1650's. Around 1730, their descendants drifted down to North Carolina and settled there. Near the Revolutionary War, my great, great, great grandfather, Solomon Ridgeway traveled west through the entire state of North Carolina and settled in Indian Territory, ...where you're sitting right now."

The contractor looked around inside the barn.

"Really?" he said with complete interest.

"This wasn't always Tennessee. If you do your research, you'll see on any old map that this was Indian Territory before they formed the state of Tennessee. As a matter of fact, if you go 75 miles east of here, you'll be in old North Carolina." Elias pointed due east. "North Carolina originally stretched from the east coast to that point 75 miles from here. When Tennessee became a state in 1796, it acquired a big portion of North Carolina and the Indian Territory. My family, the Ridgeways, owned this 100-acre plot of land that I own now. No land purchasing has transpired since Solomon Ridgeway first settled here. I own now what he owned then. My ancestor was one of the first non-Native American settlers in the area."

"Ridgeway?" the contractor asked, confusedly. "I thought that your last name was Morgan?"

"It is Morgan," Elias replied. "This farm belonged to my mother. Ridgeway was her maiden name."

"Oh, now it makes sense." The contractor nodded his head in understanding.

"This whole area since before it belonged to Tennessee was known as Ridgeway Crossing. Some of the old timers still call it that. I still refer to it as that."

"Is that right?" the contractor inquired. "I've never heard of Ridgeway Crossing."

Elias smiled, knowing that he was sharing information that only a few people in this area still remember. "You won't find it on any recent maps. The last time I believe it was ever listed as the name of this area was around the turn of the 20th Century."

"Why is that?"

"That is when the town of Fellowship was incorporated. You know, that main street with twenty or so businesses on it, where I met you."

"Is Fellowship settled on part of Ridgeway Crossing?"

"No. The Ridgeways were stubborn and strict about what they owned, and they were firm in standing ground on never selling an inch of their land."

"So Ridgeway Crossing was never incorporated into Fellowship?"

Elias continued to smile, proud that no one in his family ever succumbed to the temptations of money. "That's right and hopefully it never will be."

"Are there any Ridgeways left in the area?"

"No. I'm it."

"You are the sole survivor of the Ridgeway legacy? You don't have any close family still around these parts?"

"I've got all the family I need buried out in the back of the lot." Elias pointed in the direction of the cemetery from where they were in the barn.

"There's a cemetery back there?"

"Yes."

"Who's back there?"

"Every known descendant of Solomon Ridgeway, including old Solomon himself."

"Every single one? No one's ever moved out of the area?"

"Maybe for a short period of time, here and there... but they always come back."

"To live in the area?"

"Some of them... Most return in a box."

"To be buried here, huh?"

Elias picked up a handful of dirt from the barn floor and sifted it through his fingers. "To keep this ground pure and sacred... complete."

"Keep it in the family."

"Now you're catching on."

"So you're out here all by yourself? In this empty farmhouse?"

Elias looks around at their surroundings. "That is what it appears to be."

"Well, what happens when you die?"

It was quiet for a long, uncomfortable minute. Elias's shoulders sunk down slightly, then he spoke, changing the subject.

"Since we're done with lunch, don't you think we should probably start getting the concrete ready now? We don't want to waste the whole day."

The contractor was set back a little. "Oh... o.k. We'll have to mix by hand. I'll pour some of the mix in the wheelbarrow. Can you turn on the hose for me when I say go?"

31

"Just say when."

They both got up from the hay bales and headed in their respective directions. The contractor grabbed a bag of concrete mix from the stack over by the tools. He ripped a corner and poured it into the wheelbarrow. He picked up the hose from nearby and waved to Elias, who was by the house, to turn on the water.

Once there was an appropriate ratio of water to mix, the contractor waved again to Elias to shut off the hose. Elias stopped the water and shuffled back into the barn.

"Is that enough?" Elias asked.

"Plenty. You'll probably have to keep doing that as we get close to running out of mix in the wheelbarrow."

"Anything I can do to help."

The two worked diligently at the first layer. Elias wanted to at least be done with that part by the end of the day. The spacing of the bricks in the trench was done before lunch. The remaining task to be completed was to have a sturdy foundation setting before they were done. The contractor finished mixing the mortar in the wheelbarrow and dragged the wheelbarrow over to the trench. He started using the shovel to fill in the inside holes of the first layer of bricks to make them solid.

"Don't be stingy with that stuff," Elias said. "We can always get more. This has got to be sturdy." The contractor nodded and continued to sift the shovel over each hole until the layer was complete. This used up a good portion of the mix he had. He opened another bag and added it to the wheelbarrow.

"Elias...," he motioned towards the house with his hand.

"I'm on it," Elias shouted as he interrupted the contractor. He shambled over to the hose spigot and turned it on. The water filled the wheelbarrow almost completely, and the contractor made a "throat-cutting" motion to get Elias to shut it off. He mixed the powdered pool until it became a nice paste again. Then, he dumped the wheelbarrow into the ditch, scraping every last little bit off the bowl with the shovel. He looked at Elias.

"We have to work fast now," he shouted to the old man still standing by the house. He dumped another bag in the "mixer" and signaled to Elias, once to initiate and then again to cut the flow. He then whipped it up quickly. He dumped it again and restarted the cycle for one last dump.

Elias hobbled back over to the barn to watch over the contractor. The contractor looked up at him from his kneeling position by the wall and spoke, "Elias, you don't have to help with moving the bricks. I can take care of that myself."

"Never said I was going to," said Elias. "I'm just standing here to make sure that you do the job right."

"That's just fine," the contractor chuckled.

"So, stop staring at me and get on it."

"Yes, sir," he chuckled again.

The contractor worked diligently as he aligned the bricks and sandwiched them with mortar. He worked with precision, cleanliness, and perfect tempo. He wasn't too fast, and he wasn't too slow. He was able to work and keep a decent conversation with Elias, without breaking concentration. It amazed Elias how accurate the contractor was to the specifications that he required. Elias was pleased with his work and smiled the whole day through.

Elias and the contractor talked for hours as the day sped by. The contractor hadn't even felt as if he was putting in a full day's worth of work.

"This weather's been awful hot lately. Hotter than usual. At least, it's still dry."

Elias responded, "Where've you been, son? It's always been this hot this time of year. Ever since I was bathin' in that tin wash bucket over there, it's been like this."

"Yeah, I know. I was just making conversation. You follow the high school teams?" asked the contractor.

"Not exactly. I don't really go into town that much anymore. Besides, I was never much of a sporting type. I was always so busy with my ma, Ellen, and this farm."

"Ellen. Is that your wife's name?" he asked Elias.

"Yes, sir." Elias took a deep breath. "Her name was Ellen."

The contractor realized a little too late that he struck a nerve with his elderly employer. "I'm sorry, Elias. How long ago did you lose her?"

"Six months ago. I guess that it was just her time."

The contractor looked at Elias. "I never like to think of anyone's passing as a planned time to go."

Elias smiled, "I do believe that I agree with you."

"Were the two of you extremely close?"

"Words cannot express how close we were. We started out so differently, and somehow ended up so much the same."

The contractor was intrigued. "How's that, Elias?"

"I grew up on this farm. I never attended school outside what my dear ma taught me. But Ellen... she was a townie. She grew up in one of the wealthiest families in Fellowship. She attended school out of the county and returned to live in the biggest house in town. Ellen was never in need of a job or a chore to make her feel as if she was needed. Then, she met me, and you might assume that she would change, but she didn't. Ellen didn't have to. She was already the most unselfish, humble person I had ever met. She continued to try to convince me, even up until the day that she passed, that she was truly blessed to have met me, but she couldn't have been more wrong. It was the other way around. Without her, I could never be the man that I am today. She educated me on the ways of the world that I had never experienced. And in turn, I showed her just how hard a man, who never had more than he could fit in that tiny, old house, worked to survive. She saw me, not as the man I was before her, but as a man of courage for accepting the opportunity to culture myself without having to step foot off this property. She showed me things that I never could have even dreamed of without her guidance. And for that, I am ever grateful and love her more and more each day."

"Wow!" the contractor said. "That is amazing. I wish there had been someone like that for me."

"I'm sure there was someone." Elias got sad. "Could we possibly stop talking about her and get back to work? I've noticed that the sun is starting to set, and we were making so much progress before."

"Certainly, Elias." The contractor looked up at him and smiled again.

The two men continued on in silence for a little while, and they were making lots of headway. As it neared dusk, they were getting close to getting at least the first wall done.

The barn was dark that night. The contractor was excited about being close to finishing the first wall, so he decided late in the afternoon that he would stay late until the wall was finished. He wanted to feel some sort of accomplishment and thought it would be great to be able to start fresh on the next wall tomorrow. He told Elias about his plans and Elias agreed with his reasoning. Besides, it didn't bother Elias any. He was there alone all the time. Extended company was welcome as far as he was concerned.

Elias informed him that he would go into the kitchen and prepare something for them to eat. The contractor agreed and continued to plug away at the wall. After he heard the back door to the farmhouse slam shut, it was pin-drop quiet for several minutes. The faint chirp of nearby crickets blended unnoticeably into the night air. The miniscule synaptic glow from the tails of fireflies sporadically bounced through the barn. The moon beamed in full and strong through the cracked-open main door, but it only lit the far corner of the barn. The air was clean but heavy from the humidity still holding on through the night. Deep breaths were moistened from the mugginess and sweat steadily flowed without interruption. The contractor paced himself and slowly finished the facing side of the wall.

Constant scraping of the trowel formed a rhythmic sound, while the setting of the cinder blocks provided the bass. Soon, he would just have to set the side wall to seal off the gap. He thought it might be a good time to stop and see if Elias was ready with the promised supper. He was starving.

The contractor dropped the trowel for a moment and stood up. As he rose, he heard a solid, heavy, crunch sound come from behind him. He thought it must be Elias. At the moment he turned to confirm his assumption, a howling wind came slicing through the night air. It was the broad end of a shovel blade, and it shattered the contractor's cheekbone, knocking him unconscious in one fell swoop. With that, he dropped to the ground and a shadowed figure slowly emerged from the moon's surrounding glow. The contractor was heavy, but the shadow still managed to drag him from the center stage spotlight the moon cast on the barn floor.

CHAPTER 5

When the contractor awoke, it was early-morning. The reflective glow angled onto the contractor's face. He awoke to the sound of a nest of hungry baby birds. The typical early-morning blurriness was concealing him from the consciousness of his situation, or so he thought. The contractor's eyesight was very hazy at first, but then upon his first eye focusing, he soon realized that that he had no depth perception. When he attempted to open the second eye, he couldn't muster enough strength to do it. His left eye would not open at all, and he didn't know why. It was swollen, as was his cheekbone, forcing his eye shut. As a matter of fact, that entire side of his face was numb. The only sensation he could feel was the moisture rolling down his face and splattering heavily down onto his shirt and the floor. It wasn't sweat and it did not feel as fluid as water. It was more viscous and slow-flowing. The contractor went to reach for his face and soon realized that he could barely move his arms. Still, clouded eyes kept creeping into focus, and he began to panic. He finally gained vision in the single eye and discovered that he was not horizontal. He must have been vertically asleep for hours.

Then, it came, all at once... First thing to hit was the pain. Unsure if it was the adrenaline or the state of unconsciousness that prevented the excruciating, stabbing burn from exposing itself until now, but it became very present and very, very... unbearable. The contractor's cheekbone had been shattered, and he could not move to tend to it. It shot up his skull, on the left side, up into his brain. He screamed at the top of his lungs. What had happened?

It was just setting in now that the blurriness and the warming glow hitting his face were disguising what was a foot and a half in front of him... a cinder block. Still temporarily engulfed in mostly shadow, fear crept in, replacing early-morning obliviousness. The contractor screamed again, causing synapses to shoot through the nerves in his cheek up to the sensory section of his brain. The pain increased, so the screaming increased... which caused the pain to increase. His body convulsed as he attempted to squirm his arms into a different position. He continued to scream. Hopefully, someone would hear his yearning for help and run to his aid.

Amidst the now-tiring, extremely painful, increasing screams, the contractor heard a noise. It was quick and high-pitched, and it stopped short. The contractor stopped screaming. The sound obviously came from a door opening. It was followed by a slow-moving thud-shuffle, thud-shuffle, thud-shuffle... He could tell that whatever was making the noise was getting closer, as each step increased in volume. Then... it stopped.

It was quiet for several minutes. Then, a familiar voice cut through the air.

"I could have sworn that I heard someone screaming, but I guess I was wrong. Maybe it's just my old age sticking its tongue out at my mind."

Now, things were starting to make sense. It was Elias. This obstruction standing eighteen inches from his face was the cinder-block wall HE had built in Elias's barn. Now, he was on the other side of it, in between the outside wall and his freshly-made structure. And he was in pain... agonizing pain... but why?

"Oh well," Elias stated. "Think I'll go make some lunch."

There was a crunching sound of a pivoting foot, and the thud-shuffle began again. This time it was fading away. Should he say something? Fear of the situation had prevented him from saying anything earlier, but this was Elias. Elias was in no physical condition to get him out of there, but he could surely find help to come to his aid.

On the other hand, what if whoever put him here was still in the vicinity, just waiting in the shadows to pounce on Elias as soon as the situation was revealed? Elias seemed oblivious to the missing contractor.

Maybe he should just stay quiet until the whole thing is completely thought through and a solution could be plotted out. He could surely think of a way to get both Elias and him out of this mess. He had to hurry in decision though, because the sound of Elias's heavy feet were almost out of the barn. Elias's life was at stake as well.

"Speak or shut up," the contractor thought to himself. "What should I do?"

The footsteps stopped and the barn door began to creak closed. The contractor decided to stay silent to protect himself and Elias from imminent peril. The door creak faded and the sound of the wooden beam lock on the barn door slammed quick and hard. Then it was quiet again.

As much as it pained him to move his head, the contractor looked around in all the available directions with his good eye. Nothing appeared to be useful. Then... he looked up... and there it was. A solitary, frayed rope, full of cobwebs and swaying ever so slightly in the gentle breeze, dangling from a bowing rafter beam and glowing in the afternoon sun, now swarming into the barn from directly above him. It was a ray of light... a ray of hope.

The cinder-block wall was well constructed, and why shouldn't it be? After all, he was the one to erect it. If all else fails, the contractor could take pride in the craftsmanship of his final side job. However, it left little room for maneuverability. The way Elias described it in detail, it was meant only to keep the barn from swaying too much. It was never intended for someone to be hidden behind. He didn't think that there was any room to turn sideways, but he tried anyway to no avail. The pain he was in prevented him from doing so. He did have room, however, to try to raise his arms, elbows locked and parallel to his body. It took the contractor such a long time to get to that desired position though, because of the extreme pain he was experiencing and the limited space for maneuverability. What seemed like minutes were, in reality, hours. Every move that he made was calculated and minimized to reduce the amount of pain that he was in. He moved ever so slowly between the walls. He didn't really have a choice. Once his arms were completely vertical and in a straight line with his body, then he could twist his wrists so his palms faced outward in the direction he was looking. The cinder-block wall was ten feet tall and even with his seven-foot reach and vertical seven-inch jump, there was no way to reach the top edge of this monstrosity without assistance.

Though the top of the wall was unreachable, there was still that rope. It was dangling down at least two feet below the top edge of the wall. The contractor jumped the first time and fell two inches short of the frayed and split ends of the old rope. He kept jumping, just barely missing for what seemed like an hour. A few times, he knocked the bottom strands, sending the rope swinging like a pendulum. He stopped to rest for a few minutes and to give the rope a chance to settle out at its resting point. Every attempt at the rope sapped the contractor's energy, making the time in between tries longer and farther apart. His arms ached from being up in the air for so long. It would just waste time to put them down to his sides. He didn't have time. What if Elias had already discovered the new inhabitant on his farm and had already been dealt with? He couldn't take any more chances. He had to get out of this prison, and it had to be now.

When he was satisfied that the rope wasn't going to sway any more, he mustered up what little strength he had, closed his eyes, and he leapt to the rope. The combination of picturing himself grabbing the rope and the utter desperation gave him at least an inch and a half added on to all of his prior jumps. That final trust in himself and faith of taking a breath and just grabbing on led to success! He clutched the rope with a firm hand, and he landed on his feet. The sheer excitement, despite the enormous pain in his cheek, brought a huge smile to his face. But, the glimmer of pride was short lived. As he continued to grasp the rope, the rafter above cracked and sunk six inches.

There was no chance of that beam supporting his weight now. Regardless, he tried to apply some tension to the rope to see what capacity the wood could withstand. More concerned about the beam, the contractor failed to consider the condition of the rope, and with the added tension, the dry-rotted fibers unraveled and snapped at its weakest point. The bottom half of the rope fell to the ground alongside him, and he felt his heart drop down to his stomach.

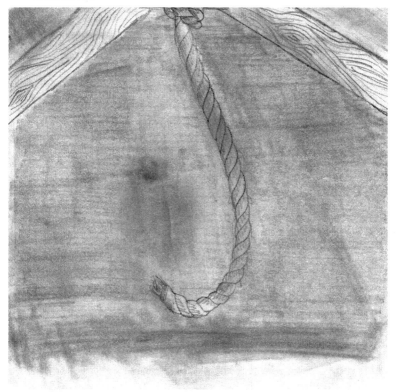

He slowly worked his arms back down to his sides. There was no point now in keeping them up in the air, and they needed the rest. As the light gracefully danced from the barn and night approached, he contemplated what could be done now.

Hours passed while the contractor considered his fleeting options. Now the barn was completely dark, and he could not see at all. The contractor was exhausted, and he decided that he would just rest for the night, waiting for the morning to draft another plan for getting out of there. It was going to be hard to try to sleep standing up, but he couldn't move enough to do anything else. The constant reminder of pain was still there as well, every time he moved his jaw, his memory was refreshed of the urgency to devise another plan to get out. His legs were numb and his feet ached from standing so long. His head throbbed from the beating it took the night before. His heart was still pounding, and his stomach was empty and growling. The sheer fact that he was still alive was amazing, but now he had to rest and preserve energy for the even bigger day tomorrow. Even though it had only been one full day, the contractor felt as if tomorrow was going to be his last ditch chance to make it out of this penitentiary. He wasn't sure just how much energy that he would have after that. He had lost a lot of blood, and with no nourishment, his doom was almost inevitable. He closed his eyes and tried to picture anything that would take his thoughts off this predicament he was in.

His body was so exhausted that it did not take long for him to nod off to sleep.

Morning came again with the sun peering in through the cracks. Groggy, but awake, the contractor heard those hungry birds again. "Why don't you shut up", he mumbled. "You think you're the only ones that are starving?" With that, he stopped and thought to himself, "I must be going crazy. I'm mouthing off to helpless baby birds!" He slowly opened his eyes. Even with no medical attention, the swelling in his left eye had gone down enough to squint through. His right eye had gained full clarity back.

He looked around, trying to remember what had happened the day before. He looked down and saw the frayed, broken rope and looked up to find the broken, sunken beam. How could he forget? Now, it was time to think. His body had ample rest, as did his mind.

He kept looking at the top of that wall. It didn't seem that far up. Sure, he couldn't jump to the edge, but maybe there was another way? What could he do? How could he get up there? Nothing came to him. His mind drew a blank. "Come on, think damn it!" he muttered. Frustrated, he leaned back and nodded his head backwards in anger against the barn wall behind him. "Think!" He did it again. "You're going to die in here!" With the third head thrust, he stopped. It must have knocked some sense into him and jarred something in the frontal lobe of his brain. "Wait a minute", he thought. He nudged his head backwards again, this time much softer. "This barn wall... it's solid. I don't know why I didn't think of it before. I guess I just assumed that the wood was old, soft and brittle. I mean, that's why the old man wanted me to build this damn, cinder block wall. He was afraid of high winds or a tornado tearing down this weather-beaten train wreck and damaging his good farming equipment. I guess he never bothered to check the stability of these walls. Well now, there's still a chance."

Hope returned to the contractor's heart, and he was eager to begin anew. First, he pushed on the cinder block wall to test it out. Then, he put pressure on the barn wall again to double check its strength. It seemed fine. The situation was perfect again. He thought to himself, "If I could just suspend myself between the cinder block and the barn and shimmy ever so slowly. First, I'll slide with my back... then, shuffle my feet... and then, continue with my back and so on. I can get high enough to grab the edge and pull myself over. I'll think about what to do next after I get over."

Eager to get started, the contractor placed his hands, palms out, up against the cinder-block wall, and he applied pressure. Locking his elbows and straightening his back, he pulled his shoulders in towards his chest, so his shoulder blades would jut out against the barn wall. He positioned his left boot on the cinder block about a foot and a half above the barn floor. Then, he pushed off the floor with his right boot and applied it to the cinder block. Now, he was completely suspended in the air. There was a slight struggle because of his weight, but he was able to stabilize himself before continuing.

"If I get out of this alive, I swear I'll stop eating doughnuts," he sarcastically thought to himself. "Doughnuts... damn, I'm hungry."

CHAPTER 6

The contractor needed to take it slowly, as this was more than likely his last chance. He didn't want to make a lot of noise, just in case the intruder was nearby. Most important, he had to be extra careful not to get any more hurt in the process. He transferred his hands higher onto the cinder block, and then he shifted his feet again, one at a time. Every advancement upward got him closer by about six inches. Every slide of his back, he could feel splinters from the rotting barn wall

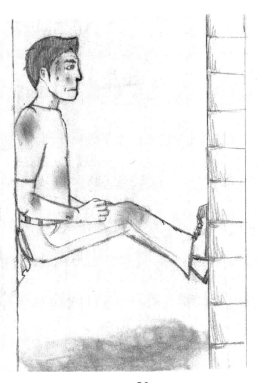

driving into him. He dared not pull away from the wall to reposition himself. That would risk a shift in his balance. He struggled on, wincing through the pain, striving for the edge of that cinder-block wall.

Thirty minutes into his ascension, he paused to rest and re-evaluate the path of his journey. Still not removing his appendages from contact with the wall, the contractor's arms and legs ached tremendously.

He kept mumbling to himself words of encouragement, "Halfway there... don't give up now... got to keep pushing."

He looked up. Roughly, three feet separated the top of his head and the top edge of the cinder block. He was getting excited now. Things were finally starting to look promising. If he could just raise his arms above his head, then the ledge would certainly be reachable within two more feet of movement. He did not want to chance his survival on impulse. He continued to keep his elbows locked and his arms three inches apart, extending from just below his ribcage and just above his stomach. He had found his center of balance and any drift away from that would certainly result in a journey-ending fall.

His rest period had to be over now. It wasn't really like resting anyway. The constant pressure outward from his body continued to add more strain as time progressed. It was unbelievably awkward to maintain this position, and it was causing his muscles to reach total fatigue rapidly. No, this rest period was more for psychological composure and next-step critical thinking.

The contractor began his routine again. His mind was set not to digress from this pattern. Left hand up... right hand up... left foot up... push back up when right foot comes up. Repeat. As the top edge of the cinder-block wall neared, he never once cracked a smile. Determination was driving him, and the face he was making, a combination of grimacing pain, fear of the immediate future, and fortitude, was almost as strong as his will.

At this point, it wasn't good enough to just grab the wall ledge. The contractor had to push most of his top-heavy upper body above the height of the wall lip. If he had just grabbed the edge and hung free from his arms, the adrenaline would have stopped aiding his arms in supporting his body. The muscles on his arms would have weakened to the point of collapse, and he would never have enough strength to pull himself up to the top of the wall.

Another thirty minutes had passed. He could now reach, if he chose to, and taste freedom. He inched slowly and could peek ever so slightly over the horizon of bricks. Every movement upward, the tension in his mind began to lift, and his thoughts began to drift. The contractor's mind flew through bacon and eggs at the town diner and the meatloaf that Elias was supposed to serve him two nights ago. He could feel his stomach stutter at the thought of just smelling food again.

Now, he was chest level with the wall top. He had to strategize how he would get his legs up and over. Still, he kept thinking about fresh ground coffee. Maybe Elias could make him some once this incident was over.

Elias! For the entire climbing expedition, he had forgotten about Elias. Oh, he hoped Elias was all right! After what the intruder had done to him, he could only imagine what kind of shape Elias would be in if the intruder had returned after yesterday's visit to the barn. The contractor looked down to see what kind of footing he could shift onto and sidestep over the wall.

Just then, he heard a sound of the barn door creaking open! It was opening ever so slowly, but the contractor couldn't stop it. He had to act impulsively to elude whoever it was at the door. He hadn't even heard the wooden beam come off to unlock the door. He was in no position yet to hop over the wall. His feet were just positioned all wrong. Besides, once on the other side of the wall and on the ground, there was just no obvious place to hide immediately.

"What if the intruder had returned?" he thought.

There was no time to rationalize a solution. Purely on instinct, he did what anyone else with no other options would do. He dropped down and grabbed the lip of the cinder-block wall. His body was like dead weight now and his muscles were like gelatin. The sheer force of his body, when his arms fully extended, pulled down with such momentum that his already-bruised fingertips could not maintain grip, and he was thrust to the ground. Since the contractor had reacted so spontaneously, he had no time to brace himself or position his body to cushion the fall.

The first part of his body to accept the impact of the solid barn floor was his right foot, twisting and snapping at the ankle. This caused a shift in his position, and he landed abruptly on his right hip. Shoving his left forearm into his mouth to keep from screaming, he endured the instant pain until the door ceased to creak.

The late afternoon sky was winding down for the day, and this was now almost the end of day two of his captivity. The barn was growing dark now, and it was quiet. The contractor sat, unable to move, waiting for the next sound. He was dripping sweat, half from the climb and half from the fear. The impact had jostled him around, and he was now in an awkward position. There was dead silence. He sat only for two minutes in silence when the door creaked again. There was never any sound in between, so whoever had been there never set foot in the barn. They must have just peeked their head in to look around and leave again. It was only one of two people: the intruder or Elias. He couldn't take the chance, though. He just sat there thinking about how close he was to freedom. Now, he may never get out. So much for those bacon and eggs...

The next morning, the contractor awoke lying to his right, full of pain in his right hip and right ankle. He must have passed out from the pain, but now it was telling him that it was time to get up again. He sat up as best he could, only to feel stabbing sensations shooting through his hip. He dropped back down again. He decided that the only way he could get up to a vertical position again would be to actually roll over so he faced the barn wall. Then, he could attempt to stand up by shifting all of his weight onto his good ankle and good hip. Once he was up on his feet, he could try to turn around to face the cinder-block wall. If he could not turn around by standing, he would have to lay back down on his bad hip, fighting through the pain. Then, he could roll over again, this time turning himself to face the cinder-block and stand up on his good hip and ankle. It was a little tedious, but he had no other option. He couldn't support all of his weight on his bad side.

He was able to get to his feet, and he soon discovered that it was impossible to turn while standing.

"Typical," he mumbled. "Always have to do things the hard way."

The contractor had to think about his next move. He couldn't fall back to the ground to roll over. He would end up on his bad hip and ankle, and he'd never get back up. After running through options in his head, he settled on a painful, but possible route. He had to back up into the cinder block wall as much as possible, and try to rotate with his belly digging into the splintered wood of the original barn wall. There was no other way. He pushed back on the wall as much as possible and suck in his stomach. Rotating slowly, he pushed through the pain. Finally, he was facing the right way. He stood there for a while, catching his breath and contemplating what his next move would be. By now, the swelling over his left eye had gone down almost completely, but his cheek still hurt like hell. While rolling on the barn floor, the frayed rope was underneath him, leaving rope burn across both his arms. Now he had a belly full of splinters. He was in really bad shape, but he was alive. Starving, but alive.

As he stood there, an odor drifted into the barn through the cracks in the wall. It was a good smell. Someone had been making breakfast. Even though he couldn't eat anything and just the smell was killing him inside, this was a good sign. How many intruders do you know that stick around and cook breakfast? This meant that Elias was still alive, and he was in good enough shape to cook some French toast. Maybe the intruder was gone long ago, who knows? If Elias was still alive, then the contractor had a chance of survival. Surely Elias could help or at least get help. "Elias probably doesn't even know that I'm here, stuck behind this wall," he thought to himself. As he finished his thoughts, there was another creak at the barn door.

Once again, there was that shuffle-step across the barn floor. It had to be Elias this time. The contractor called out to him, "Elias, is that you?" He hadn't really spoken out loud in a few days other than mumbling, so his voice was somewhat low and cracked.

"Who's there?" Elias asked.

"Elias, it's me. I need your help," the contractor replied.

"You're still here? I thought you had left me days ago. Where are you?"

"You might not believe me, but I'm stuck behind this wall that I built."

"Were you building it from the inside? I didn't think you were that stupid," Elias claimed.

"No. Someone put me here. I was hit in the face with something and the next thing I know, I woke up behind this wall."

"Like a shovel?" Elias said. "There's one laying on the floor here with a blood stain and a big dent that kind of looks like you."

"That's probably it", said the contractor. "Thank God that you're all right!! I was so worried about you. I'm just glad that you're safe. Did you hear anything suspicious three nights ago?"

"This farm has been quiet for the last ten years, but especially the last six months, you know, since Ellen died. I haven't heard much of anything besides crickets and the occasional night owl since then."

"Whoever it was remained quiet, hidden in the shadows. I only remember hearing one crunching sound after you left for the house. I thought it was probably you. When I turned to talk to you, slam! That's when he hit me."

"Are you all right back there?" Elias asked.

"Not really. Besides what I believe is a broken cheekbone, my back has splinters dug in deep, my arms have severe rope burns, my right ankle is probably broken, and my right hip may be cracked. Not to mention that I haven't eaten for two full days and I'm starving."

"How did all that happen? I thought you were just hit in the face?"

"I kept trying to get out and every attempt resulted in getting hurt."

"Isn't there <u>any</u> way you could have gotten out?"

The contractor replied, "I was afraid to at first, but then I tried several different ways to get out and something always happened. I was so close yesterday, and then I heard a noise and fell from the top of the wall."

"That must have hurt. You should have tried to at least fall on this side of the wall."

"There was no time", the contractor remarked. "Besides, I was afraid that the intruder was still here, just waiting for me to get out and finish off the job."

"You keep mentioning this intruder", Elias stated. "Did you see what he looked like?"

"No, I didn't. You know what? Could we talk about all this later? I am in a lot of pain, and I'd appreciate it if you'd help me get out of here."

"I'm afraid that I can't help you there."

"Oh, that's right. You have trouble walking from the house to the barn. How are you going to help me get out of here?"

"Have you tried kicking out the old barn boards in the wall behind you? They've been there since the barn was built over a hundred and twenty years ago."

"That's right!" the contractor exclaimed. "Why didn't I think of that? I was so busy with intricate details that I didn't bother to think of the simple and the obvious."

With that being said, the contractor stood firm on his left leg. He was going to have to kick with his bad ankle and hip. He had no other way to support himself. He felt around with his foot for what felt like a soft spot in the wooden wall. He braced himself, leaning on the cinder-block wall, and taking a deep breath, he bit his bottom lip in anticipation of the pain. He closed his eyes and raised his right leg through the crippling pain in his hip. Knee bent, he swung backwards hard and strong. There was probably only going to be one shot at cracking the wood. It would have to snap enough to make a big enough hole that he could work with. Once the hole was there, he could sit down on his good side and rip away at the wood with his hands.

His eyes scrunched, causing pain to shoot through his cheek. His foot landed solid on the wall and there was a loud crack... but it wasn't the wall. His ankle had snapped completely and his foot dangled loosely from his leg. The joint had completely shattered, and he let out a scream. It was so loud and long and deep that the birds in the orchard outside flew from the branches in fear. Anyone a quarter mile from the farm would have heard it. His face turned bright red as his skin pulled tight against his skull. Tiny blood vessels in his cheeks popped leaving splotches all over his face. The contractor felt to the ground on his bad hip and let out another blood-curdling scream. His throat was almost numb. Just then, Elias spoke.

"That's right. I forgot. I had you move my tool shed right behind that wall, didn't I?"

"What?!" the contractor shrieked.

"You know. I wanted to stabilize the tool shed as well, remember?"

The contractor sat there, writhing in pain, when suddenly it came over him. He paused while still holding his ankle and he sat there... thinking... arguing with his own mind. Back and forth... back and forth. As the thoughts spilled through his head and onto the barn floor, he forgot about the pain for just a brief moment. It was in that moment that clarity and vision came shining through. Finally, the truth settled in and the contractor's face turned from a painful scowl to an angry disgust. A calmness came over the contractor.

Gritting his teeth, he asked Elias, "You didn't forget that little tidbit, did you? You had me move that shed there on purpose, didn't you?"

"Of course, I had you move the shed there. I couldn't possibly do it, could I?" Elias answered.

"That's not what I meant," the contractor growled. "It was all strategy, wasn't it?"

"Strategy for what?" Elias questioned.

"You're behind all of this."

"All of what?"

"Tell me the truth, or prove me otherwise."

"How can I prove it to you?"

The contractor was getting angrier and angrier, as the thoughts continued to fill his mind. "Make a phone call. Find someone that can come help get me out of here."

"I'm afraid I can't do that."

"You can't... or you won't!"

"Can't... Phone's been dead for years," Elias replied.

"You're lying!"

"Try it yourself. See if I'm lying."

"Get in your car, Elias! Go and get me some help!"

"Can't... Out of gas."

"Take my truck!" The rasp in the contractor's voice, strained his throat now.

"Oh... I planned on it." He could hear the smile rise on Elias's face as the tone in his voice changed.

"What are you going to do, Elias?" he yelled. "Are you just going to leave me here behind this wall to die and rot away?!"

"I knew you weren't a complete idiot," Elias sneered.

The contractor started to realize that maybe Elias was going to get away with this. He stopped screaming and he started taking long, deep breaths. He tried to think of another way out of this situation, but there wasn't any.

"Elias."

"Yes."

"Why... Why are you doing this to me? ...Why am I here behind this wall? ...What did I ever do to you to deserve this?"

"I think that you know why you are here."

"No, I don't. I have no clue as to why you've done this to me. How could I possibly know why?"

Elias sat quiet for a moment. You could hear the smile leave his face just as quickly as it arrived. After two minutes of silence, he spoke. "You, sir, have been slowly killing my wife over the last twenty years."

"What? Before last week, I've never even heard of your wife... What was her name,... Ellen?"

"Don't ever speak that name again. You, sir, do not deserve the right to have that name pass across your lips, ever again!" Elias shifted from his calm demeanor to disgust with the thought of the contractor speaking about Ellen.

"How, then?" The contractor paused in confusion. "How did I possibly kill your wife?!" The contractor, at this point, was a ball of so many mixed emotions.

"Do you remember those nice conversations we had over the last week? Do you?"

"Vaguely. I remember you saying that your wife had been distraught over your daughter."

"The last twenty years she had been depressed over her."

The contractor was so confused with what Elias was saying. "What does that have to do with me?"

"Does the name, Sarah Morgan, ring a bell?"

"Not exactly, Elias. Should it?"

Elias tried to return to calmness despite the loathing caused by the contractor's unfamiliarity with whom they were discussing. "Sarah Morgan is my daughter."

"So?"

"Twenty years ago, my daughter, Sarah, was dating a young man. She never really dated much, and to her, this man was very, very special. Sarah fell in love with this man, and she never really told us much about him. She would go to town on the weekends and spend the entire weekend there. She would come home alone and never say a word. We never met the man, but we knew that if she thought he was wonderful, he must have been a one-of-a-kind."

"What does this have to do with me?"

"Shut up", Elias snapped. "Did I sound like I was done?"

The contractor didn't make another sound. Elias was holding all the cards now.

Elias began again. "This went on for six months. Every weekend. Sunset on Friday to sunup on Monday. Then, one Saturday, I got up at the crack of dawn, as I always do, and sitting at the kitchen table was Sarah. I was stunned. I hadn't remembered her leaving the night before, but I didn't expect her to be sitting there that morning. Ellen and I were ecstatic to see her, but we questioned why she was home."

The contractor could hear Elias sit down on an empty crate. He heard him let out a huge sigh, and it was quiet for another minute. "She said that she was home because her boyfriend told her on the phone last night that he had something to do this weekend. Her elbows were leaving grooves in the table top and her head was buried in her hands. We could tell that this was bothering her greatly. She claimed that this was unlike him to have something else planned. He always stopped what he was doing to make time for her. That weekend went by very slowly. She sat up in her room for most it, never coming down for a meal. We had to bring the food up to her, and she still barely ate any of it. The following week went by with lightning speed, and we were back to the weekend again. Friday night came, and the phone rang again. Two weekends in a row now, her man had called to cancel their plans. She was in tears the entire weekend. Normally during the week, she wouldn't call him. She said she wanted to give him his space. She didn't want to drive him away. That just made the weekends even more special for her. The second week, however, she decided to call him. She was starting to worry about his intentions and his feelings for her. Every phone call got the answering machine.

Every phone call never got a return. Friday arrived once again, and the phone didn't ring until 9:00 in the evening. He was calling yet again to cancel, saying he was sorry that he had other things to handle and that he couldn't make it. This was the last straw that Sarah could handle. She had become accustomed to traveling into town to see her boyfriend, and now, she was struggling to grasp this new inconsistency. It pained her to go for six months to see him every single weekend and have that yanked away from her cold turkey."

You could hear the sadness in Elias's voice. He was doing everything in his power not to break down and cry. "Sarah decided, without telling us, that she was going to go into town to see exactly what was biding his time. She took my car and left an hour after getting the phone call. She must have driven for hours looking for his truck. It wasn't parked in any of their usual spots. She finally drove past the only bar in town and saw the corner of his truck, tucked away behind a crowd of other cars. She pulled over and went inside to find him. He was sitting with his back facing the door. Slouched over a row of beer bottles and a pretty young woman at the end of the bar, he was obviously trying to make some moves on this poor, little girl. She never approached him. He never even knew she was there. She turned to the door and shoved through it with great force. Once in the parking lot, she hopped back in my car, slammed the door, and broke down into tears. She must have cried herself to sleep. The next morning as Ellen and I came down to eat breakfast, Sarah came walking in the back porch door. Her hair was disheveled as were her clothes. Her eyes looked puffy and red, and she was heading directly upstairs. I stopped her and sat her down at the table. She told Ellen and me about the shocking night she had just experienced. She talked about how embarrassed, angry, depressed, and lovesick she was all at the same time. We tried to comfort her as we always used to when she was still a child. She showed her appreciation for our concern, but she told us that she needed to be alone. She went up to her room and stayed there for a week and a half. We left her alone as we had promised, as much as it pained us to pass her room and hear her sobbing for hours. We gave her the space that we felt she'd needed. Then one day, she came down from her prison and sat at the breakfast table with us. She seemed better. Sarah informed us that she had made peace with what had happened to her. She claimed that now it was over, and she would be a stronger person because of it. Ellen and I were so encouraged with her change in attitude, and we were glad to have our Sarah back. We continued the week the way we used to, finishing our chores and spending time in the living room listening to the radio. We were a whole family again."

Elias stopped again. He sounded indifferent now. No smiles... no tears... no change in tone... just dry and slow in response. "What came next was not expected. The next morning, Ellen and I awoke in a good mood. We hadn't felt this way in a long time. Sarah's depression brought the mood of the whole house down for a long time. That morning was the start of a new phase in our lives. Ellen and I both had tension lifted off our shoulders from the time we opened our eyes. We sat at the table in the kitchen, waiting for Sarah to come down from her room and join us for breakfast. We waited a long time. The food was getting cold and we weren't getting any replies, so I sent Ellen upstairs to get her. Ellen told me to go ahead and start eating. I hadn't even finished my toast yet, when Ellen came running down the stairs screaming. 'Elias! Elias!' she yelled. 'She's not up there!' I dropped my coffee cup to the floor, shattering it to pieces. I jumped from my chair and ran out the back porch door. The car was still sitting there. I tried to calm Ellen. 'Maybe she went for an early morning stroll to clear her head,' I told her. Still nervous, I could see from the look on her face that she was trying to calm me down as well. 'I certainly hope so,' she said and returned to the kitchen to let me sort out my thoughts on my own. I yelled to her, 'I'll take a walk to see if I can find her!' I began to walk down the long gravel driveway, heading out towards the road leading to town. There was no sign of her. I got about two miles out on foot and decided to turn back around. I thought to myself, 'Maybe she took a shortcut through the fields. I probably just missed her.' Even twenty years ago, I was no spring chicken, so walking for that amount of time wore me out. The trek back took a lot longer than the first half of the journey. I was exhausted. When I arrived back at the house, it was well after lunch time, and I had to stop to catch my breath. Then, I called to Ellen, trying to stay calm, for her sake, to keep her sane. 'No sign of her. She'll be back before supper though. I'm heading to the barn to get some work done before dark.' I heard a soft 'All right' come from inside the house. You could tell by Ellen's tone that her worried reply was uneasy. She continued with, 'You want me to make you some...,' but I had already closed the screen door behind me before she could finish her sentence. I was nervous to leave Ellen inside the house alone, but I wanted to make her feel like all was normal. I was panicking inside, but even though I knew she was too, I couldn't have her going to pieces.

As I walked to the barn, I kept thinking to myself that it wasn't like Sarah to run off without saying anything, even when she was depressed. I opened the barn door and the sun was barely shining in through the door. It was already late in the day because of the time I spent walking around searching for Sarah, and I hadn't gotten much work done. I started putting the tractor motor back together that I had begun the week before. I worked for a few hours when I heard the back porch door slam and footsteps approaching. Maybe I shouldn't have left Ellen alone in the house for so long in this situation, but I was determined to keep my mind off of Sarah by working on the motor, and I got carried away. Ellen was used to being alone in the house while I worked out in the barn or on the farm, so I figured that this would be second nature for her. Once or twice, I thought about stopping what I was doing and going inside the house to check on her, but I controlled my impulses, because I know that Ellen would have been able to read my emotions like a psychic. Ellen had made some lemonade, and she brought out the pitcher with two glasses of ice for her and me. I heard the barn door creak slowly open as she struggled to pull it while balancing the tray with the lemonade on it. As she opened the barn door, the remainder of the sun just setting now filled the rest of the barn. And then, it happened. Ellen and I both made the discovery at the same exact time. Once light filled the barn, it exposed every corner including the west wall. Ellen dropped the tray and there was glass, ice and lemonade everywhere!"

The contractor spoke, fascinated and tense all at once, "What was in here?"

Elias looked up above the cinder-block wall to the rafters and the contractor could hear him smirk. Elias sneered back, "I see you found the rope. It was much longer last week."

He interrupted again, "I tried to use it to get out of this prison, but the rafter snapped and the rope broke on me."

Without missing a beat, Elias replied, "Well, you are much heavier than Sarah."

The contractor was in shock, forgetting all about his pain. The barn was quiet for several minutes after that. He looked up and stared at that rope. All he could think about was the image of Elias and Ellen discovering at the exact same instant that their only child was hanging from the end of a rope. He could hear muffled whimpers coming from the other side of the cinder-block. It must have finally hit Elias. That's why the rope was still hanging there. How could he honestly take something like that down? To the contractor, it was a way to get out of his prison. To Sarah, it was an escape from her prison as well. Things were slowly starting to click in the contractor's mind, but now he had questions and a story of his own to tell.

Elias didn't give him a chance though. Elias just fought through his tears and started talking again.

"I couldn't understand it. Ellen fainted from the shock. I ran to Sarah's lifeless body and grabbed the nearby ladder. Without a thought, I climbed up and loosened the noose from around her neck and carried her down the ladder. I laid her body on the barn floor near Ellen's, and sat there looking around for some answers. I turned back to the corner of the barn where the rope still hung and noticed a sheet of paper lying on the floor directly underneath. I scurried to the note, picked it up, and started reading."

Elias pulled a crinkled up piece of paper from his flannel shirt pocket. The contractor could hear him unfolding the paper and sliding his glasses onto his nose. He began reading:

"Dear mother and father... I know that I told you yesterday that things were better now. To be honest with you both, I have made peace with what has happened recently... but there are too many reminders in this world to keep my mind at bay. My life has been affected to a point that I cannot return from. I try and try to block out images... memories... feelings, but I can't find the strength within me to stop. I was addicted to being in love for so long that when the truth was finally revealed, I could not repair the damage. I know how this is going to affect you

both. I know that your love for me is strong and that this is going to tear you apart, but you must understand how much more pain and suffering you would have gone through with the stress of my life burdening your shoulders. I know that you would have accepted this added weight, but I also know how it would have strained your health. I feel that I cannot go on pulling you down with me. This was the first man I've ever loved, and it will be the last. I'm writing you this letter so you can understand why I'm doing this. I could not go without leaving you satisfying answers. Lack of closure would be just the same as continuing to live with you the way I have been living. I'm not saying that I do not want you to mourn for me. I can accept the fact that you will. I do, however, want you be able to move on with your lives. I want you to remember me fondly and keep me in your thoughts and hearts forever. I love you both very much. I hate having to leave you. Please don't hate me. I just can't honestly bring another life into this world of... "

Elias stopped reading. The contractor could hear the paper crumpling as Elias pulled his hand to his face and began sobbing.

"You!" Elias yelled out. "You are to blame for this!"

"Why?" the contractor exclaimed. "Why do you think that he is me?"

"The day after this happened, I was sorting through her room... remembering Sarah... crying over her... punching holes in her walls. I opened a box tucked away on the top shelf of her closet. Sitting right on top of the contents of the box was a notebook. I picked it up. I didn't even have to open it. Scribbled all over the cover, like a little schoolgirl crush, was your name, plastered like wallpaper. I had never seen or heard your name before that. You are the only man that has ever been in Sarah's life... and you were the last."

The contractor tried to think of something... anything that could change this situation around. From the second that Elias had mentioned his daughter's name, he knew that he was in the wrong. He remembered Sarah fondly. He never realized what his infidelity had done to her or her family. He had never even met Elias or Ellen. Back then, he didn't want to meet them. Once he was done with Sarah, he never wanted to hear from her again... And he never did. Now, he knows why.

He tried talking to Elias, "Twenty years ago, sir, I was a married man. My wife has since left me, but I was married at the time."

"I don't care what you were at the time", Elias murmured. "You were everything to Sarah."

The contractor had been cheating on his wife with Sarah. He told his wife that on the weekends he was doing odd jobs for extra money. He went on for six months this way, getting away with it the whole time. After six months, however, the wife was getting extremely suspicious about the lack of extra money appearing in his bank account. He couldn't uphold the charade any longer. He had to break it off with Sarah... quick and final. He didn't think that she would take it that hard. He didn't know that she was completely smitten with him. He thought she felt that it was just a fling, just as he treated it. And he didn't know that he had fathered a child. The shock of everything that Elias had revealed to the contractor grew in intensity the more that was exposed, but that last little tidbit was the icing on the cake. The contractor was in so much astonishment that he didn't really know how to respond. "A baby," he muttered under his breath. He shook his head in disbelief but also to clear his mind and focus on the task at hand. He had to keep Elias on track and not digress from his plan to get free from behind this wall.

"All right, all right," the contractor stated. "I remember Sarah. Yes, I was that man that she spent weekends with. I treated her like a queen for six months. I led her on. I never told her that I loved her. I never told her about my wife. She must have thought that I was just as in love with her as she was with me. I never thought that Sarah was serious about anything we had together. I thought that she was just having fun and letting things happen as they came along. I never knew that she was pregnant. If I had known, then things may have been different." The contractor hung his head, humbly in shame. "I was getting to the point where my wife was getting suspicious, so I just tossed Sarah to the side without considering her feelings. I'm sorry for that. I'm sorry that I treated her like garbage. Please... "The contractor began to cry. It wasn't a fake, "I'm saying that I'm sorry to get out here alive" cry, either. It was more of a desperate, sincere, "I know I was wrong and I'm genuinely sorry" type of tears.

But, it did not matter to Elias. "You can tell me that you're sorry until you're blue in the face. You can be as sincere as you want. You can promise me that you've changed. You can promise me the world. The one thing that you cannot promise me is that I can get my wife, my daughter, and my grandchild back."

"I know... I know," sobbed the contractor.

"Shut up," said Elias. "I really don't want to hear from you anymore."

"Why did you wait so long to do this? Twenty years is a long time. I would have thought that you'd given up or forgotten by now."

"Give up? Forget?" Elias questioned. "You're asking me to forget something that changed my life forever? This... has been in the works for twenty years.

The only reason I waited this long... was Ellen. Every day after Sarah left us took a little piece from her. She tried to put on a happy, copasetic face. She didn't have the strength to hide it. On the day she died, she looked up at me in her last moments and said, 'I have to forgive him now. I cannot pass with that on my conscience. Promise me you'll forgive him, too? We'll be waiting for you, Elias. The four of us (you, me, Sarah, and the new baby) can be happy again.' With that, she closed her eyes and whispered, 'I love you, Elias'. And then, I lost her. The last one left to love left me here. After that, all I could think about was you. Ellen was gone. Nothing I did could burden her now. I finally had the opportunity for closure. And now, it's complete. I feel it, don't you?"

"You're just going to leave me here to die?!"

"Did you ever hear me tell you that I wasn't? Do you really want me to lead you on? I wouldn't want you to feel like my Sarah did. It's past the point of no return now. If I let you out, I would go to jail."

"If you let me out, I promise you... " cried the contractor.

Elias interrupted him, "If I let you out, I promise you I'll kill you."

The contractor snapped back in anger, "I'd like to see you try! C'mon, let me out. You can TRY to take out all your anger on me. We'll see what happens." The contractor was trying to see if the old man would fall for the bait. He also gave one good push on the cinder-block wall just to make sure that his construction wasn't flawed. He was proud and disappointed all at the same time.

Elias said, quietly, "You see, that's the difference between you and me. I don't have to let you out to kill you. You can just stay where you are. You're already dead."

The contractor was quiet. He did feel it. It was over. The plan had failed. There was no use in talking anymore. He was just too weak now. He hadn't eaten for days. The adrenaline was leaving again, and the pain was returning. Elias had won and he had lost. He truly had remorse for what he had never even given a thought to twenty years ago. Maybe he should have done something about it then, but he didn't know that Sarah was pregnant with his child and that she had killed herself. He never heard anything about her again after he left her. He wanted to scream, but no one would hear him. He was nine miles out of town and screaming would only make Elias feel more satisfied. It was time to give up. He had given it his all. It was time to rest. He sat down on his good hip and closed his eyes.

Elias said his final words to the contractor. "I'm only saying this so I can join my Ellen and my Sarah... I forgive you. I forgive you for your insensitivity and your incompetence... for your selfishness and your greed. I forgive you for all the pain and suffering you've brought to this family. Intentional or not, it had an impact on us... and now, it has an impact on you. I forgive you for every tear dropped in this house and on this farm. I forgive you for every heart that was broken in this barn. I forgive you on behalf of my beloved wife and daughter. I forgive you in the name of the Lord. Finally, I forgive you for everything... yet I forgive you for nothing. This was never about revenge. This was about an incomplete circle that is now filled in. And now, I am whole."

Elias walked over and closed the barn door behind him. He put the beam down across the door and limped off into the house and stayed there for the remainder of the night.

CHAPTER 7

The next morning, Elias awoke early. He was up out of bed, had a shower, and dressed with clean clothes by 8:00. He made a complete breakfast with eggs, bacon, toast and coffee, and he ate all of it. He actually had an appetite now. It was like a whole new Elias. He had a different mindset now. Weight was lifted off of his shoulders, and he actually felt relieved. He felt good about the day ahead, and he was going to make the best of it.

He shuffled out of the kitchen, through the back porch door, and he headed towards the barn. He pulled the door open, letting the sun flow in like a wave crashing on the beach. He stepped into the barn and called out loudly, "Is anyone still here?" He had a happy tone in his question. He listened intently for anything. There was a soft, shifting sound from behind the wall, but there was no reply. "Don't worry," Elias said. "You don't have to say a word. As long as I hear something, I know you're still here... and that's good enough for me!"

He shuffled out of the barn and went over to the contractor's truck. He opened the driver's side door and slid in onto the bucket seat. "Nice. I could get used to this." He slammed the door shut and started the truck. He turned it around and backed it into the open door of the barn. He held his head out of the window. "Don't this truck sound 'perty'?!" he shouted out. He stopped the truck and got out. He went over to the other corner of the barn, opposite of the cinder-block wall. Elias pulled a dusty sheet off of a compressor and a paint sprayer. He went over to a breaker box and flipped a switch. Then, he flipped a switch on the compressor and shot a couple of paint sprays onto the dusty sheet. "Good thing that I cleaned this thing out the last time I used it."

He dragged the hose and sprayer over to the truck and sprayed a few lines on the passenger side quarter panel.

"First, we'll prime it. Then, I'll coat it with a nice, dark, inconspicuous color like dark blue. I've always liked blue."

Elias heard a little more shuffling from the behind the wall.

"Pipe down back there. It's gotten so a man can't think anymore."

He placed a ladder by the windshield on the passenger side and proceeded to tape off the glass. He covered the mirrors and the remainder of the windows. He took off the license plates and threw them in the corner. Then, he grabbed the paint sprayer and started priming the passenger side. Before long, he had the whole truck primed.

Elias took a break to go in the house for some lunch. He was so happy to have his appetite back. He cooked some of the leftover bacon from breakfast and made BLT's. The smell emigrated from the house through the barn cracks and down to the contractor. There was no fluid left in his body to salivate. His stomach felt like it was being stabbed. It was almost his time. Elias wasn't about to set him free. The contractor never even bothered to open his eyes this morning. It took every piece of strength in him just to breathe. Giving up was now the only option.

Elias finished his lunch and returned to the barn. He listened again at the wall. "You're whole truck's been primed now. It looks good, too. I'll come out tomorrow and start the top coat." The contractor listened for Elias to leave, but he didn't. He heard the shuffle-step, but he heard another noise as well. Elias was dragging something towards the wall. He heard the sound settle out and then, he heard Elias's footsteps. Elias was climbing a ladder. Then from up above, the contractor heard Elias speak.

"I was going through some stuff last night, and I found this. I thought you might like it." Over the top of the wall came something light, floating like a feather to the ground near the contractor's hand. "It's a picture of Sarah. If you can see it, it's from the second week you guys were dating. Open your damn eyes and look at the smile you stole from me."

The contractor spidered his fingers across the ground, reaching and feeling for the photograph. Sensing it, he clutched it slowly with his hand and brought it within two inches from his face. He opened his eyes gradually, squinting to focus on the picture. Barely seeing her face brought a half-smile to his. With that, he dropped his hand back to the ground, turned his head to the side, and closed his eyes one last time.

Elias shuffled down the ladder and put it back by the truck. "Guess that's it, then." He walked back out of the barn and slammed the door shut.

The next day was Thursday, and it came and went in a heartbeat. Elias finished off the paint job on the truck in spurts. He would paint a panel or two and then stop for a meal. By the end of the day, he had a brand new truck. "Just got to wait until she's dry." Elias never even bothered to check on the contractor. He was too busy with the truck. He went to bed that night dreaming about his new vehicle.

From then on, Elias never set foot in the barn again other than to park the truck, and he didn't even do that religiously. Half the time, he parked the truck out by the house now. He had no need for the barn anymore. It only brought back bad memories. He sealed off the door and put a padlock on it, for safety's sake of course. Didn't want anyone to be poking around where they don't belong. You never know who might come snooping someday. The only time Elias would even pass the barn now was to go and visit Ellen and Sarah in the back lot. He was satisfied now with his old life.

That Friday night, Elias took the truck out for its "inaugural" spin. He drove into town, filled up the tank, and drove back home. He didn't want to test the waters out too early. No one saw him other than the gas station attendant, and that was a good thing.

He kept up his usual routine of staying home at the farm for that whole weekend and the week to follow. The next Saturday rolled around, and Elias, who couldn't stop thinking about the truck that whole week, decided that it would be o.k. to finally take it out again. This time, he did not wait until sunset. He got up from bed, showered, brushed his teeth and got dressed. By then, it was already mid-morning, but Elias made up his mind that he was still going to go into town for breakfast. Extremely excited to show his face in town again, he scooted through the back door of the house and hopped into the seat of the truck. He grabbed the steering wheel with both hands, circularly rubbing it to get the full feel of sitting in the driver's seat of this beautiful truck again. He started it up, pulled down the driveway, and turned onto the main drag into town.

Even though he was so excited to go into town, he took his time, driving ever so slowly down the road. He wanted to savor every moment of steering through the countryside. As he got close to town, he passed by Henderson's fruit and vegetable roadside stand. Old Man Henderson wasn't around anymore, so his grandkids were running the stand. Even though they had no idea who he was, he waved at them and yelled out, "Good morning!"

They waved back with smiles on their faces. As he passed by, they looked at each other and shrugged their shoulders.

Elias could hear the eggs frying and smell the bacon in his mind. His mouth started to water as he entered the city limits of town. He passed by, honked his horn, and waved at the sheriff's deputy sitting in his squad car at the bank parking lot.

"Hey, Huey!" he shouted.

The deputy, shocked to see Elias out and about, pulled out of the bank parking lot and followed him to the flashing stop light at the town square. He bumped his siren once to get Elias's attention, and Elias looked back in the rear-view mirror. He pointed to Elias in the mirror to pull over in front of the resale shop. Elias pulled over and parked the truck, shutting the engine off. He looked back in the side mirror to see the deputy pulling in behind him and getting out of the squad car.

He followed him in the side mirror as the officer approached Elias's driver's side window.

Elias looked up at the officer with a smile. "Morning, Huey. How've you been?"

"Morning, Elias. I've been good."

"Can I help you with something this morning? I don't think I was breaking the law driving into town. I never have been much of a lawbreaker, especially with my driving."

"Naw, you weren't breaking any laws, Elias. I was just surprised to see you in town. I haven't seen you since... "

"I know, I know... Since Ellen died."

"Yeah. How have you been doing? Like I said, I haven't seen you in a while."

"I've been sitting at home, doing a whole lot of nothing. Just sitting there, feeling sorry for myself."

"Missing Ellen?"

"Yep."

"She always seemed to brighten everyone's day around here. We're all a little sad without her around."

There was an awkward silence for a minute, then the officer spoke again. "What brings you into town?"

"Last night, I sat in a chair in the living room, as I do every night, feeling sorry for myself. I decided to read some inspirational scripture from the Good Book, like I know Ellen would have wanted me to do. As I sat there reading, I could feel her hand resting on my shoulder. I felt good, and I felt as if she were watching over me. This morning I awoke early. I had been dreaming of her all night. I got out of bed with a smile on my face... and I was motivated. I got cleaned up and decided to come into town for some breakfast. It's just been a good morning, you know?"

"Yeah. It has been." The deputy's eyes drifted from the conversation with Elias. He gazed at the vehicle Elias was driving, from tail light to head light. "Hey, Elias. Didn't you have an old beat-up car you used to drive?"

"Yes."

"Is that old thing still running?"

"It probably could start up, but I wouldn't want to risk driving it even this little amount into town."

He looked up and down at the vehicle again. "Is this your truck?"

"Yes, sir."

"I don't believe I've ever seen you driving this thing. You always had this truck?"

"No, sir. I obtained this from my brother when he passed away a few years back. It's been sitting in my barn for a year and a half."

"Oh... That makes sense. That explains why I've never seen you driving it. Your brother must have never driven it anywhere."

Elias got a nervous tone in his voice. "Why do you say that?" he asked.

"Well, it looks like a brand new paint job. You say it's been sitting in your barn for over a year? The paint job's beautiful."

"Thank you," Elias slipped out without thinking.

"Thanks for what?"

"Thanks for the compliment. That means I've been doing my job keeping it nice for my brother. I've had it underneath a tarp in the barn to keep the dust off of it." Elias sighed in relief. "That was a nice recovery," he thought to himself.

The deputy looked at his watch. "Well... the day's just wasting away. I better get back to my post at the bank before the sheriff spots me wasting the taxpayers' money. It was good to see you again, Elias." He tapped on the truck window sill with one hand and waved goodbye as he walked back towards the squad car.

"Yeah," Elias yelled back. "It was good to see you too, Huey!"

Elias waited until Huey had started up his car and pulled a U-turn to head back to the bank before restarting the truck. "That was a close one," Elias muttered out loud as his heartbeat slowly returned to normal.

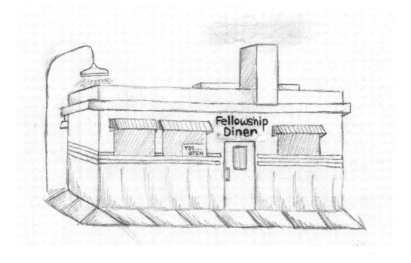

CHAPTER 8

Elias pulled up to the diner. After the conversation with Huey, now it was almost noon. Not many cars were parked in the lot alongside the diner. There were the few regular early risers that were still there, though, already finished with their meals, but had nothing else to do today. Elias shut off the truck and sat there for a minute. He hadn't been in this diner since Ellen took him out for his birthday two years ago. He was very apprehensive about entering the diner. What would people say? All the excitement and eagerness he had this morning just dropped down into the pit of his stomach. "Well, I guess I just have to jump in and get used to the water," Elias muttered. He reached for the door handle of the truck, when all of a sudden, "Wham!" Something hit the truck! He twisted his

91

torso completely around, looking back towards the direction of the noise.

It was a teenage boy walking with what appeared to be his girlfriend down the sidewalk. The boy struck the fender to get the old man's attention. As the two strolled past, the boy looked in the cab of the truck and pointed at Elias with both hands. To Elias, they appeared to be accusing fingers, directed at him. In reality, the boy was just being a rude teenager, showing off in front of his girlfriend, desperate for attention. Once Elias saw the boy laughing, he realized what was going on. He smiled and got out of the truck.

He yelled at the boy, "You got a problem touching other people's property, son?"

The youngster approached Elias in a rebellious manner, "Yeah. I can't seem to stop... See?" He started touching the driver's side fender of the truck.

A fire lit behind Elias's eyes and the boy saw it. Elias grabbed him by the front of his shirt and slammed him against the truck with both hands.

"You see...," Elias said. "You see I have the same problem."

The lad struggled to no avail. Elias held his ground.

"You know, if I was just twenty years older...," Elias laughed.

The boy was confused, and he snapped back, "Don't you mean younger?"

"Nope," smiled Elias. "If I was twenty years older, I could still kick your ass."

The boy's girlfriend, who was shocked at first, snickered. The boy looked at her, embarrassed. "Why don't you shut up, Ashley!"

Elias shook him by the shirt. "Don't talk to her like that! Maybe I'll just hold you while she beats you up." Elias smiled at the boy's girl, and she smiled back at him.

The boy looked back at Elias. "What do you want, old man?"

Elias let go of his grip and pushed the kid off his truck. "Respect."

Rudely, the kid retorted, "Sorry. I won't touch your truck anymore."

"You had better change your attitude towards people, son. There are a lot of people out there that are younger than me. If I can do what I just did, you can only imagine."

The boy settled down. "I'm sorry, sir."

"That's better. I'm sorry I ruffled your shirt."

"I guess I deserved it. I was just trying to look good in front of my girl."

Elias chuckled, "Don't you think you owe someone else an apology?" He nodded towards the girl.

"Right," the boy understood. He looked at his girlfriend. "Sorry, Ashley."

"It's o.k.," she answered.

Elias reached into his pocket and pulled out two dollars. He slapped it into the boy's hands. "Why don't you take this... and go buy her something to drink?"

The youngster smiled, "Thanks, old... I mean, sir." He walked away holding Ashley's hand. Ashley turned and looked over her shoulder at Elias.

Elias winked at her and she smiled.

Elias felt good. He smiled as he entered the diner.

As he approached the bar stool, he nodded silently at some of the familiar faces as they looked on in amazement. He straddled the stool and sat down.

The waitress, Sharon, approached Elias slowly from behind the bar. "Elias Morgan, is that you?"

"Do I know you?"

"Yes, sir. It's Sharon Hunter."

Elias looked confused. Sharon noticed.

"Sharon Hunter. I went to school with Sarah."

"Oh, yes. I'm sorry I didn't recognize you. My age runs smoke rings around my memory. You haven't always worked here, have you?"

"No, sir. I'm just part-time."

"What happened to Edna?"

"She still works here... just not as much. I fill in for what she misses. She's getting up in age, too, you know."

"Right. It's been a while since I've been to town. Things have changed a little since then."

"I and... most of the diner noticed your little skirmish out there. Is everything all right?"

"What... that?" Elias said pointing towards the window out front. "That was harmless and innocent," he said.

"It sure didn't look harmless from where I was standing."

"Who asked you to stand there? We were just having a little 'hands-on' conversation. That's all. I was demonstrating the importance of showing respect to your elders. At first, he was having trouble understanding, but... " Elias raised both of his fists. "I brought along my interpreters."

Sharon laughed. "He is a little punk. That's Riley Austin's grandson, Tyler."

Elias looked surprised. "Riley Austin. Now there's a name I haven't heard in a while. I'm awfully grateful for that, too. No wonder I didn't seem to like that kid."

Sharon nodded in agreement. "Can't blame you for saying that. Seems to be a family trait, no?"

"I see that you're familiar with them. I feel confident with you backing my story if something ever arises from it."

"Since you're here, would you like to eat? It's a little late for it, but maybe some breakfast? Or lunch?"

Elias joked, "You know, that was my only reason for coming to town this morning."

"Great. What can I get you?"

"I've been smelling eggs and coffee for a long time. I miss my wife cooking for me."

"How do you want them?" Sharon asked.

"She used to fry 'em. Over medium, I think. Cream and sugar for the coffee, too."

"Comin' right up. Anything else?"

"Yeah. When you're free, I'd like you to come sit back down and keep me company while I eat."

Sharon looked at him, sadly. "Sure, I'd like that. Keep in mind that I've got customers, though."

Elias looked around. "Hell, they can get their own coffee," he quipped.

Sharon smiled, then turned and headed into the kitchen.

Elias smiled and looked down at the local paper, sprawled out across the counter in front of him. It felt good to have someone make him breakfast again. He hadn't eaten well since Ellen passed. Loneliness filled the spot where the need for food once stood. Without the companionship of a respectable person, he was losing weight from lack of sustenance. Only once in a while did Elias make a meal worthy of being even considered a meal, and he only did that to remember Ellen and the meals that she made for them. Even during the stretch of time spent with the contractor, he couldn't eat, because he knew who the contractor really was, and the emptiness wasn't satisfied.

Sharon didn't fill the void that Ellen left, but she seemed to give him a sense of calmness, and he felt comfortable around her. It allowed him to rearrange his priorities for once and concentrate on himself. Satisfaction of the end result from his interaction with the contractor pushed him out the door this morning and sent him into town. Reacquainting with Sharon gave him the strength to finish a good meal. Ellen still left a space unfulfilled in Elias's whole sense of being. But, that would never change. Elias knew that. He just needed to rebuild himself as a whole person now. The first step was a physical restoration. Reconstructing his appetite would start the chain reaction, pulling the other aspects back into reforming him as the man he once was.

He smiled as Sharon returned with his breakfast. She placed the plate and coffee cup in front of him, looking him in the eye.

"I'll be back as soon as I finish catching up with my other customers," she said. "Stay here, even if you finish eating."

"I've got nowhere else to go right now," Elias bantered back.

When Sharon returned, she sat down on the stool next to Elias. She looked at Elias and started talking. "So Elias, where have you been?"

"What's that supposed to mean?"

"I'm just asking because I haven't seen you in a long time" said Sharon. "Actually I don't think I've seen you since... you know."

"I think it was Sarah's funeral. It has to have been at least twenty years now."

"Sorry. I didn't want to bring it up. I know it brings back painful memories."

Elias smiled at her. "Most of my life consists of painful memories. If I didn't talk about it, I'd have nothing to talk about."

Sharon smiled back. "As long as you're o.k. with it, I won't feel so bad. Earlier today, you mentioned Riley Austin. Did you have some sort of falling out with him?"

Elias chuckled, "Falling out? We were never 'in'. From a very young age, Riley's taunted me throughout my life. When we were young, he used to wrestle with me, and I got pushed in the mud a lot. The other kids were always following him around. As we hit our teens, he was always trying to compete with me in school. He never let up. Then, we graduated, and he and I fought over the same job in town, which he got and I was stuck back at home, working the farm. But finally, I got one over on him. Riley came from the high society end of town. He always thought of himself in the highest regards. He was always one step ahead and one rung higher than everyone else."

"I've noticed that air about him even now," Sharon interrupted. "Every time he comes into the diner, he walks past old acquaintances without an acknowledgement. He looks down on the people he passes. And he talks to everyone with utter disregard for their feelings, as long as it makes him feel good about himself."

"That's Riley, all right," Elias agreed.

"But how you did you ever get the advantage over him?"

"Many, many years ago, he and I just happened to be in town at the same time. As a matter of fact, we were right here in this diner. We were sitting at opposite ends. Riley was sitting over there with a bunch of his snobby friends." Elias pointed to a booth by the door. "And I was sitting in that booth right over there, in the corner. Wow, this brings back memories!"

Sharon could see that taking the time to sit with Elias was helping him improve his demeanor, so she just sat there letting him ramble on with his story. Every now and then, she would get up to wait on a customer, but Sharon never let him see that she wasn't paying attention to him. She could see that this was important to him, and she made sure that he knew that he was being listened and paid attention to the whole time.

Elias smiled the entire time he spoke.

"If Edna were here right now, she could help me with the story. She was right here behind the counter the whole time, you know. Anyway, Riley was carrying on and laughing loudly with his friends, and I sat there alone, enjoying my coffee and working on a crossword puzzle. The door to the diner opened and a beautiful woman entered. Riley and his chums noticed her right away and were silent as she approached the counter and sat down on a stool. She sat very erect and ladylike, which drew Riley's attention away from his pals, who had returned to their loud discussion. Riley stared at this woman, as his friends continued to talk to him, not noticing that he was ignoring them. I hadn't noticed her at first, as my back was to the front door and my attention was focused deep into a five-letter word for 'Woodrow Wilson's wife'. I had no letters in that section, and my mind was drawing a blank. I sat there, staring at the puzzle for at least another five minutes."

Elias continued. *"Riley had risen from his seat in the booth, telling his companions to move over, so he could get out. He shoved through them like baby pigs trying to find a spot on their mother to eat. He eventually got out* and stood up straight. He dusted off the sleeves of his shirt and straightened his collar. After checking the pleat in his pants, he looked up at his destination: the counter stool next to this woman. As he started walking, his snobbish swagger kicked in. Still unnoticed by the woman, he slid onto the stool next to her, spinning slowly so his back and both elbows rested on the counter and he faced opposite of her. She gave him a once over and without a second thought, looked back at Edna."

"I don't remember the whole beginning because I was still doing my crossword, but Edna told me what transpired that day many times. She said that the woman clearly had no interest in Riley before he could say one word to her. Edna just stood there, watching.

The woman said, 'Excuse me, Edna? Could I have a slice of that pie on the counter and some coffee, please?'

Being the outspoken person that Edna was, she responded. 'Not to be rude, but how exactly do you know my name? I have no idea who you are, and I think I would remember.'

'It's on your nametag.'

Edna was embarrassed, and she didn't say another word until the pie was on the plate and the coffee cup was in front of her. 'I'm so sorry.'

The woman smiled, 'No harm done.'

Riley was still sitting there, quietly waiting for his opportunity to grace her with his proficiency in wooing a

101

woman. *This was his shot to make his move. 'Best pie for miles around.'*

'So I've heard,' she replied.

Riley looked over at me, struggling with words to say. 'Look at that loser... over there. All alone. Just sitting there, oblivious to the world around him and content with the constant company of himself.'

The woman looked at me and then looked back at Riley. 'He seems focused on what's important to him. He's complacent with the simple things like a cup of coffee and a newspaper. He doesn't look like he needs companions to feed his ego. I admire that.' She smiled at Riley, knowing she put him back in his place.

Riley knew that he had blown it with the woman, so he slithered away from the counter and approached his compadres, who were now all staring at him and his rejection. He had to do something to save face. As he got closer to his friends, he muttered, 'Prude'. They all laughed and nudged him, showing him acceptance back in the group.

At this point, I was getting frustrated with this clue in the puzzle, and I noticed that my cup was empty. I turned to grasp Edna's attention for a fresh cup of coffee, and it was then that I noticed her. She was already looking at me. It seemed as if she had been staring, intrigued and waiting for me to turn to get a glimpse of my face. At least, that's what Edna told me. She was very beautiful,

102

very prim, and very proper. She was way out of my league... and I couldn't help but stare back at her. I noticed over her shoulder that Edna was staring at me, too. I shook my head to clear my thought and called Edna to bring me some more coffee. I turned back to the direction I originally faced. I was embarrassed, and I couldn't look down at the paper. I closed my eyes and listened, taking deep breaths. It was quiet for that moment between my booth and the counter, although the diner bustled about around us. Then, a squeak from the stool broke the silence I was experiencing. My chest started to ache, as I heard the click of high heels slowly approach my table. It obviously wasn't Edna. Could you imagine her spending the day juggling plates in heels? My eyes were still closed, and I heard the footsteps stop behind me. The faint scent of lilac perfume flew up my nose, and my heart sank. I took a deep breath and turned as if I didn't even hear her approach. 'Edna, my coff...?' As I spun my torso, my eyes drifted up into hers. I was speechless.

She was nervous too, although I never noticed. I just sat there until she spoke. 'I-I noticed you were working diligently on a crossword puzzle. I'm pretty good at them. Could we share it?'

I was in awe. She was a beautiful, crossword-puzzling, sophisticated woman wanting to spend time with me. Me. Of all people.

'Sure,' I said. I couldn't think. 'Have a seat.'

'Thank you.'

Edna came over to the table, smiling. 'I take it you'll be finishing your pie over here.'

The woman looked up at Edna and Edna winked back at her. 'Thank you, Edna.'

As she looked down at the crossword puzzle, I couldn't take my eyes off of her. She smiled, nervously, and pointed at the puzzle. 'Ellen.'

'What?' She had startled me out of amazement.

'Ellen... a five-letter word for Woodrow Wilson's wife. It's Ellen.'

'Oh... Oh great. I was stumped with that one. It was on the tip of my tongue.'

'That's where a name like that should be.'

I was confused. 'Huh?'

'I'm sorry. I was just saying that I would like to hear you say that name.'

'Which name?'

'Ellen.'

'Oh, right.'

'That's my name.'

'Which name?'

'Ellen.'

'Oh, right... right. Oh, right! I get it. I'm sorry. I'm just a little nervous. My name's... '

I couldn't think of my name. I was starting to sweat. Edna came up to the table and topped off our coffee cups. 'Elias,' Edna said.

'What?' We both looked at Edna.

'Elias. It's your name.'

'Thank you, uhh...'

'Edna.'

'Right. Thank you, Edna.'

'I'll bring you some more pie... on the house. You both look hungry. Keep working on your puzzle.' Edna scurried off to the counter again and returned with two big hunks of pie. She smiled at the two of us, and we both nodded our gratitude to her.

And that was it. We spent the rest of the night in that booth, talking about all sorts of things. When the diner closed, I walked her home with never a silent moment between us. It wasn't until we stopped in front of her house and I realized where she lived that I finally shut up. She was high class, all right. From her attire to her speech to her neighborhood, she was upper crust. She was interested in me, though. And from that point on, that's all that mattered. For the rest of our lives, that's all that mattered to me. She loved me for who I was. And that's how I finally got the best of Riley Austin."

Elias hadn't been paying attention to the time or the fact that Sharon was still there. He got so caught up in his story that when he was done, the little hand on the clock had spun a half of the face. Sharon was staring at him in complete attention with her chin in her palm and tears semi-smeared across her cheeks. She smiled at him, but said nothing. Elias couldn't think of anything else to say either. He was all talked out. He smiled back at her and spoke.

"Wow. I'm sorry I wasted your day just rambling on. I speak very slowly when I get caught up telling a story. I just don't want to leave out anything," Elias said.

"That's quite all right, sir. Judging by the looks across the room, I'm not the only one to have enjoyed it," Sharon commented.

Elias looked around the diner. More than one regular either nodded their head or tipped their cup of coffee towards him. And Sharon wasn't the only woman having trouble staying dry-eyed. Elias nodded back at most of them with a smile before looking back at Sharon. He grasped her hand before rising from his stool. He could feel his back seizing up as he stood up straight, but Elias never lost the smile on his face. "Thanks for listening to an old man reminisce. I had better be going now. It's getting late."

Sharon stood up from the stool. "Elias, that story was amazing. Thank you for sharing it with me. It was an honor listening to you. Anytime you feel like talking, just come back in and I'll be here. You be careful going home now." Sharon walked him to the door of the diner and held the door for him. "Good night, Elias."

"Good night, Sharon." Elias smiled as he walked towards the truck. It wasn't completely dark yet, but Sharon had no one to close up tonight, so she was closing up early. Sharon locked the diner door behind him and turned off the OPEN sign.

Elias sat in his truck for a few minutes before starting it. He just kept thinking and smiling. He wasn't thinking of the kindness of Sharon, but Ellen. If Ellen hadn't been so kind to him so long ago, just imagine what kind of life he would have lived. He finally started the truck and pulled out onto the highway for home. Even with his slow pace driving, with his wandering thoughts, he was home before he could even remember driving there. Darkness now engulfed the farm. He got out of the truck, went into the house, turned off all the lights, and went straight to bed. This was going to be a good night for dreaming.

CHAPTER 9

Elias woke that Sunday morning, sitting straight up in bed. He couldn't recall what he had been dreaming, but he had an uneasy feeling in the pit of his stomach. He stepped out of bed onto the cold, hardwood floor, and rushed into the bathroom. After using the facilities, he hopped straight into the shower. Something in his mind was urging him to get moving. He scrubbed himself clean and stepped out to shave in the mirror. Although he hadn't used it in a while, his straight razor was still as sharp as ever. He took off a year's worth of beard in a matter of minutes. After slapping on some really old aftershave from the medicine cabinet, he headed off towards the bedroom closet. Normally, his everyday clothes were folded nicely and placed in his dresser drawers. He would grab a full outfit for the day, and there would always be at least one more for the next. His drawers were empty now. The person who normally filled them was gone, and he never bothered to try it. In the closet, however, his good clothes hung, fully pressed and in plastic covers. They were very rarely worn, so they remained in their proper state for many years. Elias hunted through his best suits, searching for the very best one. When he found it, he nodded his head and removed the suit from its dust-covered preservation. He got dressed very quickly.

Elias grabbed a plain-colored tie from the closet doorknob and fixed it properly underneath his collar. Pulling a comb that had been in his suit pocket, he plowed through his still-wet hair, grunting through knots, and wincing in slight pain. He hobbled down the stairs into the kitchen and proceeded to make himself some toast and coffee. Careful not to get any crumbs on his good suit, he finished off the toast and downed the hot coffee. He kept looking at his watch that hadn't worked for at least eight months now. He didn't know why he kept putting it back on. It was just routine. He could stop off later and get a battery for it.

Elias hobbled out the back door quickly and hopped into the truck. He started the truck and put it into gear in one motion. Circling around, he headed up the driveway and onto the main highway into town. Where was Elias going in such a hurry? He sped down the highway and just near the outskirts of town, he slowed down. He didn't want to run anyone over so close to town.

He was still moving at a good pace. Elias didn't want to be late. If he walked in late, it would only draw more attention to him than he was already going to get just by showing up. His mind drifted to the scenario that was about to occur. Apprehensive already, his stomach soured with the thought of the next ten minutes. He was so distracted that he almost took out a rabbit crossing the road in front of him. Noticing the creature at the last possible moment, he swerved drastically to avoid the poor, little thing. Just missing the rabbit, he slammed on the truck brakes and looked in the side mirror, only to see the frightened, little animal scurry off into the brush alongside the road. He caught his breath and sat there for a moment to settle his racing heart. Elias thought to himself about how horrible it would be to take the life from something... Oh, right... again. His thought returned to his purpose for leaving the house this morning. Looking ahead through the windshield, he spotted his destination, one block up, on the corner. Still unsure of the time, he finished his voyage and parked the truck. Turning off the engine, he cranked the window down to listen. There he sat... in the church parking lot... listening for any sound. Before he could finish cranking down the window, he heard it. The choir, as small as it was, sang out clearly through the open church windows.

He was late. Today was the one day that Elias didn't want to be late for anything. As much as he tried, he just barely missed it. Anyone else would have no problem coming in late to Sunday service. It just wouldn't stir up any controversy. But for Elias, it was different. If he entered the doors of the church late, the service would probably cease, then and there. A silence would come across the congregation like a tornado in an open field. Elias would be the one person in this town that could do that. He hadn't been in the presence of the Lord since Ellen had passed. Even before she was gone, he still had not been a regular congregant in a long time. And when Ellen passed on, Elias had said some pretty harsh, malicious words in front of and pertaining to the entire congregation. In so many words, Elias had accused Pastor Jones and his flock of drawing Ellen away from him. All the time she had spent doing things for and with the church was time that he didn't have with her. He pointed fingers at people that called upon Ellen for social church gatherings and Bible study groups. He was resentful, bitter, and jealous of each and every person in that church body. He even spoke against the Lord for taking his Ellen away from him. As selfish as it sounds, Elias knew deep down that it wasn't true. He let his emotions speak for him without thought for the consequences it might bring. Those who really knew Elias and Ellen personally could see through this fit of rage and knew that it only came from the pain and anguish of losing the most important person in his life.

There were those, however, that Elias looked down upon that did not know him and could not understand his accusations and his insensitivity towards them. Those people were the ones that Elias was afraid could not forgive him. He sensed this when he started coming

111

back into town. At the grocery store, the hardware store, and the diner, he got stares from all directions. Most people in this town knew him. Hell, most people in this town went to that church. The number of people that he offended was probably pretty close to matching the population sign posted just outside the city limits.

And for this, Elias was remorseful. At first when he came home from Ellen's funeral, he felt justified in his active rampage. A few days had to pass before he would stop pacing the living room floor, arguing with an invisible debater, defending his speech given in that church. He finally calmed down and as he sat there continuing to think about it, other feelings settled in. He thought to himself that maybe the others weren't to blame at all. Maybe Elias was just trying to give himself an excuse for allowing the loneliness and emptiness to hold him down.

Elias was originally thinking about the times he would miss with Ellen in the future. He didn't stop, until that moment, to cherish the abundant memories that filled his past. When he finally did realize what kind of fulfilling life that he did have with Ellen, he broke down and sobbed for at least a few hours. He was crying with good memories and bad, but also the thought of what he had said to the town in the church that day. He was too embarrassed to even set foot in town until the day he found a reason. He was going to

reinforce his barn, and he needed supplies. That was good enough to send him back into the lions' den.

Now, he had conquered the fear of returning to town. He had been places all over town where his accused were partaking of the same country-fresh air that he was breathing. The only place he hadn't even attempted to enter was the church. And here sat Elias. With the window rolled down, the singing voices broke through the fall silence, but magically transformed in the air to mumbling whispers about Elias and his return to the scene of the crime. He listened as the singing stopped, and the pastor began his prayer. Yes, it was definitely too late to go in now. He couldn't just waltz in during the middle of a prayer and wreak havoc on this innocent crowd.

So, Elias sat there. He listened as Pastor Jones preached, about all things... forgiveness. Pastor Jones talked about how, if you surrender all to God and confess your sins before him, then you will be forgiven. Elias couldn't move a muscle. The words flowing through the air hypnotized him, and he held his head down as a humbled man. He thought about Ellen, Sarah, the contractor, the townspeople, everything. Each thought flashed through his mind, out one ear, circling around the cab of the truck just long enough for him to forget, and then back in the other ear, reminding him once more of his personal anguish.

Elias was so deep in thought that he didn't notice one of the regular ushers sneak out of the back door of the church for a quick smoke. The usher lit his cigarette and stared out over the parking lot. It was a beautiful autumn day and the falling leaves were covering the cars in the lot. The usher then spotted Elias. Squinting into the sun, he discovered who was behind the wheel, but the usher didn't recognize the truck. Unbeknownst to Elias, the usher snuck back into the building. Elias never suspected anything. Elias waited until the sermon was over and he heard the congregation begin to sing the benediction hymn, before he started his truck and pulled out of the parking lot. He figured that the singing would muffle the starter, and he was right. He didn't want anyone to even know that he was there today. He thought about going to the diner, but then he remembered it was Sunday. Everything was closed in town. He decided that it would just be in his best interest to go back home. Just then, it began to rain... hard. Elias couldn't understand it. It came out of nowhere. He looked up to the sky, and it was still sunny. Everywhere he looked, it was dry. The raincloud appeared to be hovering over his truck... and it was following him. He turned onto the main highway leading home. Once he left the city limits, he floored the accelerator to get home as fast as possible. Out of sight... out of mind... out of this rain...

He pulled onto the drive leading to the barn. Instead of leaving the truck sitting parked outside, he got out and opened the barn. The rain continued to pour down on him and the truck. Elias got back in, pulled the truck into the barn, and shut it off. Getting out, his gaze drifted up instinctively to the frayed, dangling rope. He shook his head in disappointment and then, he hung his head in shame. Everything around him seemed to slow as he exited the barn. He turned and looked in the barn for a moment. Then, out of sheer anger, Elias slammed the barn door, dropped the wooden beam across both doors, and slapped a padlock onto the door clasp.

He was angry now because he let his life run him instead of the other way around. Every major incident in his short seventy years left irreversible damage. There was almost nothing left of him. He had no strength left and nothing to lean on. As he entered the house, the raincloud dissipated as quickly as it had appeared, and Elias reflected on all the things that got him to this point. His father left. His brothers left. His mother weighed him down, piling her problems on top of his. Then, after she passed, things started to get better. He married Ellen.

In the instant that he thought of her, he hobbled quickly up the stairs and into their bedroom. He smiled wide as he shuffled over to the closet. Reaching up to the shelf above, Elias removed a heavy, rectangular box and set it on the bed. He sat on the bed and lifted the lid from the box. Wiping his finger across the lid, he made at least a half inch crevasse in the soft, dusty surface. Holding the lid away from him, he blew a year's worth of dust into the air. The light seeping through the bedroom window shade made it appear as if a blizzard had hit only in the bedroom. Breathing in the dust, he coughed strong for a couple of minutes until he could clear his throat.

Elias peered into the lidless box and grinned. He reached in and hoisted a heavy, well-protected photo album in pristine condition. He sat the book on his lap with a grunt. Opening the front cover, he could hear the binding crinkle from lack of use. This album had been forgotten for so many years. The first page started with pictures from the third chapter of his life. The first chapter was his early childhood before his father left. The second ended with his mother's death. This chapter was a renewal of the life that he never had originally. This marked the arrival of Ellen. He didn't have any pictures before that. No one cared enough to take any or preserve old ones, but that was o.k. by him. He didn't want to be reminded of those times. He wanted his pictorial life to start here, and he was so glad that it did.

Elias studied every picture on every page carefully, remembering what it was like to actually smile. Ellen started putting this album together several years ago, only finishing it a few months before she passed. She had consolidated her mountainous stacks of photographs from their life together and composed this

117

masterpiece. Each page was chronological, starting with their first <u>official</u> date. Every birthday, every holiday, every life-changing event was in this book. He spent a lot of time staring at their wedding photos.

It was a beautiful summer day when they got married. They got married right here on the farm, out behind the house. There were about a hundred guests. Most of them were friends or family of Ellen. The only ones to show up from Elias's side were his brothers and their spouses. Any time there was a party or free food, they were there. Otherwise, they were like ghosts. They left him to take care of his mother on his own. They only appeared if something was in it for them.

Elias's dad never knew anything about his wife or his brothers' families. He didn't care to stick around when they were kids so why should he get to know his in-laws or grandkids? Not that he would care anyway. He didn't even show up when the woman he left alone with three children passed away to pay his respects. He had a new family and his first one didn't count anymore. It's almost like he and his brothers were a practice family. You know, this would warm him up for the big leagues. He chose to give himself a do-over. Elias and his siblings didn't even exist anymore.

Anyway. Elias's wedding was simple, but beautiful. All of the guests were seated in the barn with the doors held open. Chairs faced the door, looking down the driveway to the huge, willow tree opposite the house. Josiah Preslar, the local tri-county winning fiddle player, softly played the wedding march as Elias and Pastor Jones stood beneath the tree, waiting for Ellen to emerge from the farmhouse. She was beautiful. The door slowly opened, and she floated out of the house. Draped in a flowing, snow-white gown and a paper-thin, mesh veil, she gracefully crossed the driveway in her bare feet and approached the two awaiting her arrival. Ellen wasn't much for wearing high heels. Clinging to her father's arm, you could see her smile from under the veil, and you know that this was meant to be.

Her father liked Elias, and he thought that he was a fine, hard-working person that would be a good provider for his daughter. A tear rolled down her father's cheek, not just because of the loss of his only daughter, but because he was gaining a son much like himself. Her father shook Elias's hand, and he passed his daughter from his arm to Elias's. Then, he quietly backed away into the barn to leave them alone with the pastor.

Elias put down the photo album and got up from the bed. He went over to the window and pulled up the shade. He looked out and down to the driveway. He could see the spot under the tree where they were wed. He imagined himself down there on that day. There they stood alone. It was just them and Pastor Jones.

They requested everyone to stay in the barn and watch from a distance. Ellen thought it would be more private that way. They couldn't hear the pastor speak or the vows Elias and Ellen said to each other. People were still there but they had to sense what was being said. The guests could see how much they loved each other without being distracted by the ritual words. It was really quite beautiful, and a lot of people were emotionally moved. Elias and Ellen didn't have to concentrate on the guests at all... just each other. After the vows, Ellen threw her bouquet of fresh flowers, picked that morning from Elias's garden, into the crowd of women. Widow Henderson caught it. She died four months later. What a waste!

Then, the party began. The barn was all done up for the celebration. The guests danced and talked and drank and ate and laughed all night long. It was a feast for all. Most of the church congregation was there. In fact, more came for the party than those that came for the wedding. All these people were there for Ellen's funeral as well. The same people Elias yelled at and pointed a judging finger at were all at his wedding... but he was happy then.

Elias sat back down on the bed and picked the album back up. He made it through the end of the wedding shots, and then he came across the birth of Sarah. Ellen had taken pictures of everything: first smile, first word, first tooth, first lost tooth, first solid food, first crawl, walk, bike ride, driving lesson. It was all there. Page after page, Sarah... Sarah... Sarah.

There were pictures of Sarah with Elias, with Ellen, with every person from that church, friends from schools, meaningless boyfriends... everyone. Every squad, troop, or team she was ever on was in that book. As she got older throughout the pages, the amount of people in the pictures with her slowly dwindled until it was either Elias, Ellen, or a solo photo. You could tell by the subject of the photo what stage Sarah was going through at that exact moment in time. As Elias turned each page, his mood got deeper and darker. He finally reached the last page of the album, and he started to cry. It wasn't a trickle of tears, either. It was a realization-of-being-alone heavy sob. He stopped crying long enough to rip the last page of the album before throwing the book on the floor. He ran from the bedroom, clutching that page in his hand and sobbing heavily again.

CHAPTER 10

Several hours had passed, and it was pitch black outside. He hobbled down the stairs and ran over to the cupboard. Elias was still clutching onto that picture. Opening the cupboard and moving some glasses, he found what he was looking for: a bottle of homemade wine that someone gave him at Ellen's funeral. He pulled it out from the cupboard and uncorked the bottle. Elias brought the bottle up to his nose first to make sure it was still good. It smelled alright. Strong, but okay. He took a swig in his mouth straight from the bottle and swirled it around his tongue. It tasted pretty damn good, too. He chugged some more and went into the living room to sit down.

Once he was in his easy chair, he took another swig and looked at that last page, still lodged in his fingers. This page was the only one in the album that looked as if it had damage on it. Every other page was in pristine condition. This page, however, was warped. Warped from water damage. Elias knew just how it got that way, and it sent him over the edge. He knew that there were times when he would come back in the house and Ellen was nowhere to be found. He would comb the house for her and find her up in the bedroom. Her eyes were always red as if she had been crying, but she would just be sitting there on the bed. Sometimes, she would slip up and forget to put the album away, but he would pretend not to notice. He never said a word to her other than, "Are you alright?" She would quietly reply, "I'm fine." Elias knew better though. That is how the page was ruined.

And this upset him. That's why he continued to alternate sobbing and drinking. He kept staring at that page, even while he drank. Eventually, he put down the page and the bottle. Elias rose from his chair and walked over to Ellen's bookcase. He dragged his finger along the dusty spines on the middle shelf until he found the one with the most wear on the binding. He didn't even have to look at the title. Elias knew he had the right book. It was the book Ellen read the most: the Bible.

He sat back down in the chair. He opened the book up and it just fell loosely open. There was no crunching of fresh pages. There was no spring left in the spine resisting to keep the book open. As he turned each page, they fell one atop the next as if Ellen had been casually skimming for her favorite meditation. Each page had more handwriting than type. There were so many different things written in that book: notes on scripture, questions about life, requests for prayer, statements about perseverance, faith, and love. Elias had not once ever looked in her Bible. It wasn't about curiosity or lack of faith. Elias respected the fact that

Ellen's Bible was Ellen's Bible. Although he knew that she would gladly share anything in that book with him, be it written or printed, he respected her relationship with her Bible and with God. Just as he once had his own personal connection, he didn't want to step all over hers. She never gave any inclination that he was, but wanted to be positive that he never would.

His own personal feeling about God swayed like a pendulum throughout his life. At several points, he was at both ends of the spectrum. He never truly believed that there was no God, but at a lot of moments, he had questions. As he sat there, skimming through pages, he would read Ellen's comments after each and every verse, and things started to make sense. He didn't really understand the words before, but now through Ellen's absentee teachings, he was starting to see the whole picture. Questions from long ago were remembered and then answered. Elias looked over at the bottle sitting open on the table. He replaced the cork and put it back down again.

Elias was getting tired now. He didn't know if it was the exciting morning of getting dressed and rushing to church, the disappointment of being late, racing to get out of there before anyone saw him, staring at years of old pictures, sobbing tremendously, or the alcohol. He picked the "all of the above" option. He wanted to keep reading. It almost felt as if Ellen were standing just over his shoulder, reading aloud to him. It made him feel warm inside... or maybe that was the wine. He thought, "Maybe if I just take a little nap, then I would be refreshed and I could keep reading."

Elias's eyes were heavily drooping now. He flipped through the pages quickly, looking for a good spot where he could pick up when he woke. As he skimmed, one verse seemed to pop out at him. He stopped flipping and turned back to that page. The verse he noticed was underlined, so he knew right where to look. He glanced over it and nodded his head in agreement and acknowledgement. Elias, then, laid the Bible, face down and open to the page, across his slumped chest. He put the recliner footrest up and leaned back. The last page of the photo album was still in his lap. He picked it up and looked at it. After reading some passages, this page didn't seem the same anymore. Instead of bringing tears, it now brought a smile to his face. He thought to himself, as his eyes were almost fully closed now, "What a nice image to fall asleep to."

With that, Elias drifted off into a happy slumber. The Bible remained there, over his heart, and the album page slipped from his grasp, down onto his lap.

CHAPTER 11

Monday morning came extremely early and the sun beat on old Ridgeway farm. The birds were up and the clouds were missing. Across town in the church parsonage, Pastor Jones was up and out of bed early. He showered, dressed, and ate breakfast in a hurry. He was on a mission today. His goal this morning was to herd a lost sheep back into the flock.

You see, yesterday after the church service, one of the ushers approached Pastor Jones. After retreating to the pastor's office and closing the door, the usher felt comfortable enough to divulge what he had just seen. Without explaining that he was outside smoking a cigarette during one of Pastor Jones's sermons, the usher informed the pastor about scanning the parking lot and noticing an unfamiliar truck with someone in it. After further distant detective work, he determined that it was Elias behind the wheel.

Elias had been sitting there, looking at his watch, talking to himself, and shaking his head in a negative manner. The usher noticed that Elias was dressed in what appeared to be his best Sunday suit. Elias sat there for most of the service with his window rolled down, listening to the pastor speak. When the hymns started, Elias sang right through them. As the service came to a close, the usher noticed Elias start up his truck and pull away towards home.

This news excited Pastor Jones for several reasons. Elias had found some reason to join them this fine Sunday morning. Was it that he realized that his accusations at the funeral were unfounded, harsh, and an error in his judgment? Was he there to ask forgiveness from the church, the pastor, or better yet... the Lord? According to the usher, Elias was dressed in his best suit. That means Elias had every intention of coming into the church on good terms. You don't dress up if you're not coming in or plan on making more unsubstantiated claims against innocent victims. The usher noticed Elias kept looking at his watch and looking sad, so Elias must have been late and had enough respect not to barge in and make a scene, especially if he was trying to make amends. He must have already been embarrassed from the last instance, so he avoided causing more trouble. He also left in a hurry, so no one would see him. He dodged any confrontations that he wasn't prepared for or didn't initiate. These were all good signs from Elias. It meant that he was remorseful and stepping forward to accept the responsibilities for his actions.

Pastor Jones was pleased, and he was inclined to show Elias that he understood what he was going through. He wanted to explain to Elias that it was okay

127

not to come into the church just yet. It takes time to heal, and Elias didn't have to rush into anything. The church would always be there for him...when he was ready. It was a symbol of good faith for Elias to even drive into the parking lot. Pastor Jones wanted to help ease Elias's anxiety and help him plan out his return to the church family. This way, Elias would feel more comfortable a lot quicker than if he were doing this all by himself. The pastor wanted to sit down and read some scripture with Elias to help him understand how it's never too late to accept the Lord into his life. He wanted to see him back in the church pews, but only when he was ready to come back.

Pastor Jones smiled as he left the parsonage and got into his car. It was time to pay Elias a visit this beautiful Monday morning. As he pulled out of the driveway and onto the road leading to the Ridgeway farm, the pastor tried to remember the last time he had gone this way for anything. It definitely had to be Ellen's funeral. There is nothing else out this direction. You could kill someone over here and no one would ever know.

The pastor continued on until he saw the driveway for the Ridgeway farm. He pulled in and stopped his car several feet in front of the house. Normally when coming to visit Ellen, he would pull all the way back by the barn, and knock on the back door. Out of respect for Elias, he stopped out in front to approach the front door. He got out of the car and closed the door. On his way to the front door, he admired Ellen's garden alongside the house. "Wow," he thought. "Elias must be keeping that up for her."

He walked up the crack, chipped, concrete steps to the front door. He knocked twice quietly, and he waited. There was never a doorbell, so that's all he could do. After 3 minutes, there was still no answer. He knocked again. No answer. Where could Elias be? He stepped down and walked to the driveway. Elias's old car was parked back by the barn off of the driveway and on the grass. The usher had mentioned a truck that Elias was driving. There was no sign of that. Maybe Elias wasn't home? It was still pretty early. Surely, the pastor would have seen him on the road leading to town, heading the opposite direction? The pastor hopped back up the steps and pounded on the door.

Maybe Elias hadn't heard him. After a few more minutes, there was still no response. Elias had to be home. Pastor Jones was concerned. Elias was up in age and something may be wrong with him. He came back down the stairs and walked around the house to get a better look. It was quiet out there so far from town.

As the pastor approached the back door, he continued looking at the barn. Maybe Elias was up early and in the barn. Instead of heading to the back door, he made his way over to the barn door. He noticed a beam blocking the door and a padlock on a latch. After a closer inspection, the padlock hadn't been completely engaged. The pastor was coming to all sorts of conclusions. Hopefully, Elias hadn't gotten locked accidentally in the barn. He was afraid to go further, but he had to do it. He was a leader in the community, and he had a moral responsibility to concern himself over the health and well-being of a fellow citizen and a future congregant.

The pastor twisted the lock and disengaged the latch. He struggled, but was able to muster enough strength to push the beam up and out of the way. He pulled the door ever so slightly. The barn was dark inside, except for some beams of light peering through cracks in the wall. Sticking his head around the corner of the door, he still could not see. He slowly opened the door fully to let all the light in. Now that there was more light, he could see everything. "Elias?" he called out. No answer. There was the truck the usher had mentioned, parked inside the barn. He stepped one foot inside the barn and said it again, "Elias?" He crept in closer so he could see if Elias was in the truck or under it. No sight of him. He yelled out, "Are you in here?"

There was still no answer. Pastor Jones shrugged his shoulders and stepped out of the barn. Closing the barn door, he replaced the beam where it once hung and put the padlock back in the latch. He didn't lock it, though. Maybe it was unlocked for a reason.

Pastor Jones turned and looked back at the house. "Elias has got to be home," he thought. He approached the back door and knocked on the screen door. No answer. He opened the screen door and knocked on the solid wooden door. The door had not been fully latched and it popped open slightly. The pastor was surprised. "This is strange," he pondered. Just like the barn, it was his moral duty to go inside to check on Elias. He continued to push the door open slightly as it creaked. He poked his head in.

"Elias?" He stepped inside the now fully-open door. "Elias? It's Pastor Jones." He closed the door behind him. "One of my ushers saw you sitting outside the church yesterday and he told me about it. I haven't seen you in a while." He tiptoed through the kitchen, heading towards the living room. "I just thought I would check on you."

The pastor finally made it to the living room and looked over to the recliner. He was behind it, as it faced the front door. It was reclined, and the pastor could see an arm and the top of a head. He slowly stepped towards the chair.

"Elias? Are you awake? It's me. Pastor Jones." He reached out his hand to wake Elias. He placed it on Elias's shoulder, and that is when he felt it. Elias was cold...really cold. Even in all this heat, he was ice cold. The pastor grabbed Elias's wrist and checked for a pulse.

There was none. Elias was gone.

Pastor Jones held Elias's hand and said a prayer aloud over him. He laid his hand back down gently on the arm rest of the recliner. "Better not touch anything else," he thought. "Until the sheriff comes." He went into the kitchen. "I'll just tell them everything I have touched so far, including this phone."

He picked up the handset from the cradle and started dialing the sheriff's office on the old rotary phone. Putting the phone to his ear, there was nothing...no sound at all. The pastor clicked the cradle a few times. Still no dial tone. "Phone must be dead," he thought aloud. "Guess I'll have to drive into town to reach him." He hung up the phone in the cradle and walked over to double-check Elias. "Yep," he said, "It's definite." He looked throughout the house, retracing his steps, so he knew exactly what he touched. He went out the back door and around the house to his car in the driveway. He got in, backed out of the driveway, and headed into town.

CHAPTER 12

The pastor pulled up in front of the sheriff's office and parked his car. While getting out, Pastor Jones noticed that only one of the two squad cars was parked there. He slammed his door shut and went inside. He approached the main desk and looked around for someone to help him.

Only one person was inside, too. Sheriff's deputy, Huey Scott, was sitting at his desk, enjoying a cup of coffee with his feet propped up on it. Huey noticed the pastor, but he did not budge from his spot. For most people in this town, Huey would have shown respect by sitting up in his chair. However, Huey didn't have too much admiration for Pastor Jones. He couldn't explain it. He just had a bad vibe from the pastor that never really sat right with him. He even waited for the pastor to speak first.

"Huey," Pastor Jones called out. "We have a predicament."

"That's Deputy Scott," Huey grumbled back. "What kind of problem are we talking about here?"

"It's Elias Morgan out on the old Ridgeway farm."

Huey smiled. He liked Elias. "What's old Elias done now?"

"He died," the pastor responded.

"Really?" Huey asked sadly. "That's a shame. Elias was my buddy. Sure, he was grumpy sometimes, but we got along well."

Pastor Jones didn't seem to share the sentiment. "Yes, well, he's gone now, and someone needs to go out to his house and take care of his remains."

Huey was curious. "Did you find him?"

"Yes. I left everything just as it was when I entered the premises. I made a list of all the things I touched or moved. Here it is. I figured it would help you."

Huey snatched it from the pastor's hand. "You should never touch anything in a deceased person's home. You contaminate things that help us determine what really happened. For future reference, don't touch anything."

The pastor was a little perturbed with Huey's response. "Look, deputy...I deal with death as much as you do, and I know about police procedures when it comes to people dying. I'd appreciate the same amount of respect I'm giving to you."

Huey looked at Pastor Jones, eye to eye. "You have to have respect for someone to be able to give it to them. It's not automatic. It's earned."

There was silence for at least a minute before the deputy spoke again. "Where's he located?"

Pastor Jones, still offended by Huey's last remark, waited before answering him. "He's slumped over in his living room recliner. I checked his pulse twice. He was quite cold, too." The pastor looked around the office. "Where's the sheriff?"

"He's taking a week off. If you're worried, I'm handling everything. I can deal with this. I've done it before. This is my job, you know."

The pastor was still concerned. "Would you like me to accompany you out there?"

Huey was angered greatly. Trying to keep his composure, he stared down the pastor. "Good day, sir."

"Fine." The pastor left without saying another word. He got in his car and drove back to the church.

Huey grabbed his hat and his keys. He locked the office on his way out, and he got in his squad car. He started it up and raced down the road leading out of town. Passing the church, he turned on his lights and siren, just to annoy the pastor who was getting out of his car.

CHAPTER 13

As he approached the farm, he thought about Elias. It was such a shame that Elias was gone. Elias was a good man, and Huey never had a problem with him. He knew how much Ellen's death had affected Elias, and he felt sorry for the old guy. It was a shame that he had to die alone like that.

Huey pulled into the drive, and he parked all the way back by the barn. He got out of the car and opened the trunk. Grabbing a pair of sterile, rubber gloves, he went in the back door of the house.

Huey walked through the kitchen, looking around as he made his way through the house. He stepped into the living room and found Elias. He was laying back in the recliner. He spoke out loud, already knowing the response. "Elias?" He checked Elias's pulse. Nothing. Poor guy. He stood there for a moment, looking down over his good friend. He noticed the book on his chest and the album page still in Elias's hand. He picked up the book first. It was the Bible. Huey wasn't surprised. He thought aloud, "Wonder if he knew that it was his time?" He turned the open book over and looked at what he was reading. It was open to Acts 10:43. This was the only verse underlined on this particular page. Huey could tell this was Ellen's Bible. Elias would've never had this delicate handwriting. At least Elias was reading it though. The passage read as follows:

"All the prophets testify about him that everyone who believes in him receives forgiveness of sins through his name."

"Oh yeah," Huey thought. "He knew." As he reached for the album page, he smelled alcohol and noticed the wine bottle. He picked it up and sniffed it. Looking inside, he determined that there wasn't much gone. It was quite strong, but Elias hadn't imbibed long enough to kill himself. Huey grabbed the album page from Elias's hand and turned it over to look at it. "Oh wow!" he said. He couldn't believe what Elias was holding. He stared at it for a good two minutes before putting it back in Elias's lap. It was a picture of Sarah Morgan, by herself. She was sitting at the kitchen table, and she was smiling. Something wasn't right though. You could see in Sarah's eyes a lot of pain and suffering. You could tell that she had been crying. The caption gave away the reason Elias had been clutching it when he died.

It read, "Last picture of our dear Sarah." The handwriting was the same as in the Bible. Ellen had to have put the picture in the album and labeled it. Huey was certain that if he searched enough around the house, that he would find the remainder of the photo album.

"Poor Elias <u>and</u> poor Ellen," he thought. They both died from the same thing: a broken heart. Elias's was probably worse, though. He lost <u>two</u> people so dear to him. This was not a suicide, and there was no foul play involved.

Huey took the Bible from where he had first laid it down. He walked over to the shelf where there were quite a few other books. He traced his finger along the spines until he found a gap where the Bible belonged. He closed the book and looked back at Elias.

"I hope he found what he was looking for when he needed it. Obviously, he wanted forgiveness for something." Huey replaced the book in its original spot. All of the other books were covered completely with dust, except for one. Curious, he plucked that book from the shelf.

"Must have read this one recently," he said. He looked at the title. "Interesting. Wonder why he picked this book to read?" It was a book of short stories from Edgar Allan Poe. He put it back on the shelf and looked at Elias one more time before leaving the house. "Gonna miss you, buddy."

He closed the back door on his way out. He walked back to his car, thinking about all the arrangements that needed to be made now. Elias didn't have any living kin to do this, so Huey had some work to do. He got in his car, started it up, and headed into town.

Luckily enough for Huey, the county coroner's office was in town and not some other town. He didn't have to go far. He got out and went inside. After some careful explanation about Elias, the coroner was completely filled in about what happened on the Ridgeway farm. Arrangements were made for the coroner to pick up the body and bring Elias back to clean him up for a funeral. There was no funeral parlor in town, so Elias was going to be brought back to the farmhouse for a wake and funeral. Originally, Huey thought about having Elias brought back to the church, but he remembered Ellen's funeral and how many problems Elias had with the church then. The farm was a safer bet. Besides, the cemetery was on the back lot of the farm anyway. It made more sense to do it that way.

Now that the funeral arrangements were mostly done, Huey wondered about Elias's estate. As far as he knew, there was no kin to inherit it, so he was curious how it would be settled. Huey decided to pay Hollis Woodward, the only lawyer in town, a visit. Maybe, he would know something about the Ridgeway farm.

CHAPTER 14

After leaving the coroner's office, he got back in his car and headed over to Attorney Woodward's office. Luckily enough, the attorney was not out of the office when Huey got there. Huey got out of his car and knocked on the door. After hearing a faint "come in," he opened the screen door and entered the office.

Huey walked into the attorney's office. Mr. Woodward looked up from his newspaper and smiled at Huey.

"Well, well, well...if it isn't Huey Scott? How are you, deputy?"

Huey was always glad to see his friend. He smiled back.

"I'm good, Hollis. Haven't seen you in a while. What's new in your neck of the woods?"

"I've been on vacation in North Carolina. I spent a month and a half with my nephew and his family. They live in Asheville. It was a nice little break from the doldrums of this old place."

"Sounds like fun," replied Huey.

"What brings you here, Huey? Just visiting or do you have some business for me?"

Huey was glad that Hollis brought it up first. He didn't know how to bring up the subject.

"Well..." Huey said. "Do you remember Elias Morgan?"

"Elias...sure I do. It's been about a year since I last saw him."

"Didn't you see him right after Ellen died?" Huey questioned. "That was only six months ago."

A confused look grew on Hollis' face. You could tell that he was trying to recollect. "Now that I think about, Huey, I guess you might be right about that. You know how busy we attorneys are."

"This is a decent size county, Hollis, but this town doesn't have that many people where you wouldn't remember when one of them dies, especially when you help with their arrangements..." Huey retorted.

Hollis looked embarrassed. "Right. Well, how is that old codger?"

Huey's face grew sad. "That's just it, Hollis. He's dead."

"Really? Wow. I know that he was getting quite old, but he was still in rather good shape. When did this happen?"

"The coroner was just on his way there now, but I suspect it was sometime between last night and this morning. Pastor Jones found him this morning."

Hollis was quiet. He looked at Huey. "Oh... Pastor Jones, huh?"

Huey smirked. "Yeah, I know." It seems as though most people in this town share the same feelings about that man."

Hollis replied, "Well, how can I help?"

"Elias, as you know, was all alone now on that farm. I don't know if he had any family left anywhere. His estate will have to be dealt with, and I thought maybe you could help me out with that. I figured that you're the only attorney in the area, so if Elias had ever gone to anyone about his property, it would probably be you."

"Wow. Pretty good deducing, detective," Hollis smiled.

"Not a detective, just a deputy, Hollis."

Hollis looked upward in thought. "Now that I think about it, it was about a year ago that I last saw Elias. He did come into my office. It was right after Ellen died."

Huey smiled. "What did he want?"

"Can't quite recall. However, I know that I have some paperwork around here. You can see how behind I am in getting this all sorted out. I will have to search for it and get back to you."

Huey replied, "That's fine. That actually takes some stress off my mind knowing that Elias was prepared for this. I just feel like I owe Elias that much to help him out. He didn't have many friends and he was a good man. He deserves a decent funeral and closure of his estate."

Hollis smiled at Huey, thinking back about their good friend. "When's the funeral, Huey?"

"Day after tomorrow. Still got some arrangements to take care of. Tomorrow's gonna be a long day. I have to do this in addition to my duties as a deputy. The sheriff will be back next week, so he can help me catch up on paperwork then. That'll help take some of the load off my shoulders."

"I'll try to have that paperwork for you by then. I'll be at the funeral. Will it be at the church?"

Huey looked at Hollis without say a word.

Hollis continued, "Oh right...I guess it'll be at the farm, then. I guess I've got a lot of searching to do before then. I'd better get started."

Huey turned to leave. "Hey, thanks again, Hollis. I'll see you on Wednesday." Huey walked out of the office.

Hollis yelled out through the door. "See you Wednesday."

CHAPTER 15

Tuesday came and went in a hurry. Huey went on a call about an accident with a tractor at the Holmes farm. He pulled over three speeders, two of which were from out of town. He stopped at the florist for flowers at the farmhouse. There was a stop at the monument shop to get a marker for the cemetery. Elias never had one set for Ellen, so Huey was going to get one with both their names on it. It made him feel good to do that for them.

Huey had so much to do, and he didn't want to miss anything. He wanted to put an obituary in the newspaper, but he realized that he didn't know too much about Elias. He thought to himself, "Where could I get information on Elias?" Confused, Huey actually pulled his car over to the shoulder to think. He sat there for a few minutes before it came to him. "Birth records," he said aloud. "Nah. Tennessee as a whole doesn't have a lot of old records on hand. Besides, I would need some parents' names, a birth date, a file number, an index, something, anything... How about the farmhouse? Surely, there would be some sort of record or at least something written down back at the house."

Huey did a U-turn on the highway and headed towards Ridgeway farm. He pulled into the back by the barn and parked. Getting out of the car, he forgot to shut the car door as he ran to the back steps. Fully knowing that no one was in the house, he knocked regardless, out of respect for Elias. Pausing for a second, he opened the door and entered the house.

He tried to think about where Elias or Ellen would have kept anything like that. Nothing came to mind. Frustrated, he clenched his fist and smacked his forehead a few times. "Think, Huey, think." And then, it came to him. It was almost as if Elias had whispered in his ear.

"You're thinking too hard. Think of an overall picture. Generally, where do people keep this kind of thing? Shoebox... shelf... bedroom closet... upstairs." Huey smiled and leapt up the stairs, taking two at a time until he reached the top. Running down the hall, he peeked in every door until he found the master bedroom. Stopping just inside the door, he scanned the room for the closet with a smile never leaving his face.

The bed hadn't been interrupted, so he wondered if Elias had made the bed on the morning he died. It was entirely possible that Elias had never slept in it the night before, considering that Pastor Jones found him in the recliner that morning. On the bed, an empty photo album box and a photo album sat. The photo album was turned to the last page, and it appeared as if the very last page had been torn out. This must have been the page that Huey found in Elias's grasp that morning. But why was the album upstairs, when the last page was downstairs still in Elias's clutches? Did Elias leave the album upstairs or did he bring it back upstairs later? Huey was starting to piece unsolved aspects of the case together now. He hadn't gone upstairs Monday morning. He didn't feel it to be important. It appeared to be a cut-and-dry case of age-contributing health factors that caused Elias to die that day. There was no need to explore the homestead, or so Huey thought. For now, it remained a mystery, but he wasn't going to forget this. For the time being, he closed the album, placed it back in its box, and searched for its home.

Huey found the closet and placed the album box back in its dust-free spot on the shelf. Scanning around the closet, he could not find anything that resembled a record of birth, death, or marriage. There was a hat box with a nice bowler in it and a paper bag with some old hand-made scarves, but there was nothing that could help him here. His smile slowly melted off his face and onto the floor.

Huey sat down on the bed, thinking about how he was letting down Elias. He didn't know what to do now. He thought about poor Elias, lying in the recliner, grasping that album page, with the Bible on his... "The Bible!" Huey yelled out. Sure... The Bible. He hadn't thought of that. A lot times, people utilize their Bibles to record personal family information like births, deaths, and marriages. Huey got excited again and sprung from the bed, racing out the door, down the stairs, into the living room, and stopping in front of the bookcase.

He scanned the bookcase again, using his index finger to trace the spines, looking for the spot where he placed the Bible back on the shelf. Finally coming across it, he yanked it from its resting place and opened it to the front of the book. Nothing there. Just Adam and Eve. He skimmed through the book quickly like one of those flipbooks where the stick figure on the corner of the page does an action as you advance through each page. Stopping at the back page, there was nothing there either. Disappointed again, he flipped through the Bible slower now. There were underlined passages, written thoughts and emotions, and dog-eared pages but no family records. He made it back to the inside front cover and noticed that this was Ellen's Bible. She had written her name there. He closed the book again and returned it to the shelf.

Huey was just about to turn and leave when he noticed a much-older looking book, sitting right next to Ellen's Bible. The spine had been ripped away, and the only thing holding the front cover to the back cover was the glue-covered strands from the inside of the binding. He picked it up slowly, so he wouldn't contribute to the damage of the already weather-beaten and cracked, leather-bound book. He gracefully opened the front cover, and it almost fell off. Huey caught it just in time.

It was an extremely old book, and a lot of the printed words were badly faded, but still legible. As he glanced over to the inside of the front cover, the corners of his mouth grew upward. He had found what he was searching for. In huge, handwritten letters, he read the words aloud, "Ridgeway Family Bible." His heart started to race.

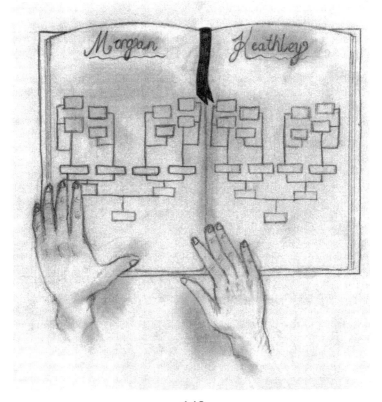

He turned each page with the utmost respect, until he got to the middle of the book… and there it was. In beautiful penmanship with what appeared to be written with a quill and ink, there was an ahnentafel leading the Ridgeways all the way back to England. On the next few pages, there was a register of every generation of descendants in the Ridgeway line, including birthdates and places, marriage dates and places, death dates and places, and burial dates and places. There was immigration information as well. It was a genealogist's dream.

Huey was amazed at all the information contained within those few pages. He slowly scanned each page until he was current with this generation. There was Elias. It was amazing to see how many different people had recorded in this book by the changes in handwriting. Elias's immediate family was the last entry in the Bible. Perusing through the dates, there was one common detail. Elias Jedidiah Morgan was the only name without a death date. Ellen Mae Keathley Morgan and Sarah June Morgan were there, complete with dates. Huey was writing all this down now. He wrote down Elias's parents' information. It was unusual because someone had drawn a thin line through Elias's father's name and dates. Huey wondered what that was all about. Elias's father was also not buried in the family cemetery with his mother. That was strange, too.

Elias also had two brothers listed: J.S. Morgan and Leroy Turner Morgan. That could have been a solution to the estate problem, except for one small problem. They were dead, too. They weren't in the Ridgeway cemetery either. Huey was beginning to see just how difficult that it would be to fairly decide what to do with the property. However, he found what he was looking for. Huey folded the paper with the names and dates, and he stuffed it into his front pants pocket. He walked into the kitchen and started ruffling through the kitchen drawers, looking for a nicer pen. In the back on one junk drawer, he found a small wooden box. He spread the items on top of it to the side and lifted it out of the drawer to examine it. He opened the box to find a calligraphy pen with refills that were still good. Huey had never written in any different style before, but he was going to try. He changed the ink in the pen and started practicing letters and numbers. When he felt comfortable with the quality of his handwriting, he slowly filled in Monday's date in the Bible for Elias's death and tomorrow's date for the burial. He wrote the Ridgeway family cemetery down, and as he finished the last letters, he started smiling again. He waited a few minutes for the ink to dry, admiring his handy-work in the meantime. When it was dry, he closed the Bible and carefully placed it back on the shelf. He looked around as he vacated the house and got in his car. He still had work to do before tomorrow.

CHAPTER 16

Huey woke on Wednesday, bright and early. It was a sad day, but he had mixed feelings about it. On one hand, a good man had passed, and today was the day to honor him, mourn, and celebrate his life. On the other hand, Huey was slightly excited. He had never arranged for such an event before. Normally, it would stop at the deputy's duties, and the family would take care of the rest. This time, there was no family to finish the second half. Huey was just anxious to see how well he handled it and what the turnout would be.

He got out of bed and raced to get ready. He showered, brushed his teeth, combed his hair, shaved, and slapped on some cologne. Now, what should he wear? Should he dress in his uniform and attend on official business? Or, should he dress in a suit and tie and attend as a friend of Elias? Elias was a good man and a good friend. He deserved more than a professional funeral. He deserved a personal one. Suit and tie it is.

Eating some fresh toast, he scrambled out the door, walked past the squad car, and got into his own personal car. If he was going to go personal, then it would be whole-hearted. He sped off towards Ridgeway farm, staying just below the speed limit. He still was a representative of the law. He got to the farm and pulled into the driveway. Already on the back stoop was the arrangement of flowers he had ordered from the florist.

He picked up the flowers and went to the back door. The house was quiet... really, really quiet. It wasn't a normal quiet, either. It was as if the house itself knew that its most recent inhabitant was no longer going to be roaming the halls. The house was honoring Elias with an extreme moment of silence.

Huey purposely left the back door to the house open. The only person that he mentioned this to was the coroner. It was important for the coroner to be able to get in if he arrived before Huey. He didn't want to leave the guy stuck in a van in the driveway with Elias's body in the back. The late summer sun would make the van get extremely hot and that would not be good. Huey was definitely smart enough to think of this beforehand, and it paid off, too. Huey was correct in assuming that the coroner would appear at the house before he did. After leaving the floral arrangement on the kitchen table and heading into the living room, Huey made a sudden and complete stop.

There it was sitting on a portable gurney in front of the living room window. Elias's coffin had the lid open, and Elias lay there in his best Sunday suit. It was the suit he was married in, and now, it's the suit he'll be buried in. Huey approached the coffin and looked down on his good friend.

Elias looked good. The coroner did a proper job cleaning up Elias's recent unkempt appearance. It was the smoothest shave Elias had had in at least six months. Make-up covered the liver spots, blemishes, scars, and bruises that Elias had earned in his old age. They were like medals achieved throughout his battle with life. Out of respect for those medals, Elias deserved to have them covered and made to look his best. His hair was combed and the glasses, which normally hung from a chain around his neck, hung there still. He never really wore them anyway, so why should he start now? Lying there, he looked ten years younger. It was such a shame that he had to die to age in reverse.

Huey grasped Elias's cold hand that had been clasped with the other and was resting on Elias's chest. He smiled at him and muttered, "You're a good friend, Elias. I'm going to remember you fondly and think of you often. Soon, this shell of your former self will be resting next to your true love. I'm sure you're enjoying keeping her company as we speak. Say hi to Ellen for me."

He held Elias's hand for one more brief moment, and then gently returned his hand to its final resting place. He went into the kitchen to get the flowers from the table and returned to the living room. There was only one floral arrangement, so Huey split it up into half-filled glasses that he found in the kitchen cabinet. Spreading it out brought a little breath of outside into this normally dreary room. It was starting to get a little warm in the house as the sun continued to rise. Huey decided to open some windows to let the open air sing through the house. Elias looked warm in that suit. Huey could tell because he sure as hell was getting hot.

Huey looked around the room to see if there was anything left to do...anything to help take his mind off the heat. Everything was pretty much done and ready for visitors...except for one thing. Huey remembered now. He walked out the front door, down the steps and out to his car. He opened the driver's side, rear door and picked up a small box from the bench seat. He closed the door and went back inside.

Huey set the box on an end table just inside the front door. He opened it up and took something out. It was a funeral card for Elias. After Huey found Elias's family Bible, he decided to stop at the print shop in town and have a hundred cards run off. Huey didn't get a chance to examine them until now. They had Elias's vital information and a nice reading of scripture on each one. Huey felt like it would be a nice touch for people to remember Elias. He smelled the fresh ink on the card and placed it into his suit coat's inside pocket.

Now, there was really nothing left to do. Nothing to distract him from...the windows...right...back to opening those windows. He grabbed some paper towels and went over to the living room windows. The sills were covered in dust. He dipped the paper towels in one of the glasses that had flowers in it, and he wiped the window panes, dusting the sills last. Trying to keep his coat clean, he removed it, looking at Elias for approval. "No disrespect, pal. Just trying to stay presentable." He smiled at Elias as the newly-found sun bounced over to the casket. "Much better," he said aloud.

Originally, Huey was going to lay some food out, but he didn't know how many would show, so he didn't bother. It was going to be a very short service after the wake anyway. He made arrangements for the coroner to come back out and help him get Elias to the back lot, where he would rest eternally. Huey was going to bury him himself. He brought spare clothes, and he could just use Elias's equipment to do the job. Elias had once shown him the rigging that was used to lower every one of his ancestors into the sacred ground out back. It seemed simple enough.

Now, it was just a waiting game. No one had shown up yet and Huey had been there about an hour and a half. All he could do was sit down and wait. He looked around the room for an available chair. Elias's and Ellen's main chairs were off limits to everyone including him to show respect for these two. There was an empty chair in the corner, so Huey sat there to wait. The clock on the wall had stopped long ago, and Huey had run out of the door this morning without his watch. He had no way of keeping track of the time.

He looked at the coffin, confused. Huey walked over and picked up Elias's left arm and rolled back the coat sleeve. Hell, Elias's watch was still ticking. Maybe he could just borrow it for today. Elias wasn't on any kind of schedule. He unclasped the band on the watch and slid it off Elias's wrist. "Sorry, buddy. I'll put it back before I close the lid." He slid the watch over his own left wrist and clasped it tight. Huey then sat back down in the chair he was already in.

Now that he was using a working watch, time seemed to drag even slower. He could feel it on his wrist, so it was a constant reminder to keep on checking it. Another hour had passed, and still no one had arrived. Huey was starting to get angry. He had gone through all this trouble and no one was showing the courtesy to even stop by for a few minutes. He wasn't just angry about that, though. What made him even more perturbed was that Elias was being punished; condemned if you will. Elias had normally been a very pleasant individual to most that had come in contact with him. He had only started getting unfriendly once Ellen had passed on, and Huey completely understood why Elias reacted that way. Now, Elias was being

157

shunned for a natural reaction to a climactic event in his life.

Huey wasn't going to allow this funeral to fall apart as it seemed to be doing. He jumped out of his chair and stormed past the coffin, looking down at Elias. "I'll be right back, Elias," he said. "I'm gonna get you the respect you deserve."

CHAPTER 17

Huey stomped through the kitchen and out the back door. He turned and locked the back door with Elias's spare keys. He marched down the driveway to his car, opened the door, got in, and slammed it shut behind him. He started the car and didn't wait for the car to warm up before spinning the tires and peeling out towards town.

Hauling down the highway, the rubber grip of the steering wheel was rubbing off onto his palms as he clenched and twisted his hands in anger. Hunched over the wheel, he scanned the sidewalks and driveways as he sped into town. It seemed as if he couldn't find one soul roaming the streets. Most of the parking lots in town were empty and the businesses appeared closed. "Where is everybody?" he yelled aloud.

Huey passed by the church parking lot and noticed a few cars in the lot. "Finally!" he said. Pulling in to park, he almost didn't wait for the car to stop before getting out. With the car door still open and the car still running, he ran up to the church door. It was locked. He jogged around the building, trying every single door until he found one open.

It was quiet inside. The lights were all off. "Hello?" he shouted, echoing down the hallway. No answer. He walked through the darkness, checking room handles and peering with his hand shading his eyes into empty room windows. Where were the people that belonged to those cars outside? Frustrated, Huey walked back down the hallway, out of the door, and back to his car. The sun was brighter now that he had been in extreme darkness. He squinted his eyes until they could adjust to the level of light outside again. Getting back in his car, he took one last trip around the town square before heading back down the highway towards Ridgeway farm.

As Huey approached the farm, he noticed a few cars parked under the shade of trees, just before the driveway. They weren't there before. He hadn't passed anyone on the way in or out of town. As he got closer, he noticed more cars parked along the highway shoulder. What was this about? Confused, he pulled into the driveway and stopped suddenly. He was amazed at what he saw.

There was no room for him to pull any further. Cars were everywhere! They filled up the driveway and covered most of the front lawn. There were at least fifteen to twenty cars and sitting at the very back of the driveway by the barn was the church bus. Every vehicle was full including the bus. Some were standing outside, either finding shade under the trees, or smoking, or conversing with each other.

Huey opened the door to the car, and holding onto the door, stepped one leg out. Still half in the car, he stood up in awe of the sight before him. His eyes were wide and his jaw was low until someone from the back by the bus broke the silence and shouted out, "Hey, Huey!" Huey smiled as he finished exiting the car and shutting the door. As he slowly progressed down the driveway, people from all directions were smiling, saying hello, extending their hands, and yet some were looking at their watches.

Huey reached the back door to find more people on the back steps, including Sharon from the diner. He approached her. She stood up and smiled at him. Fixing his tie for him, she said, "Been waitin' on you, officer. Where've you been?"

"I was out looking for all of you. How'd I miss all of you?"

Sharon replied, "I have no idea. We've only been here about twenty minutes, though. We all drove together like a caravan. We were all at the church."

Huey was confused. "Why were you all at the church?"

"Well, Pastor Jones was upset that we weren't having a church service for Elias. He traveled through most of the town yesterday, explaining to everyone why Elias said what he said and why he reacted that way. He convinced us that it was only fair to have a church

161

service for Elias. He explained that Elias wasn't a bad man and that he didn't deserve to be punished for anything, although most of us knew that anyway. Pastor knew that Elias didn't want to be presided over in the church, so he arranged for an informal service as a remembrance to him."

Huey was still somewhat confused. "Why didn't anyone tell me? I was around town all day yesterday making arrangements for this."

"Pastor Jones must have been two steps behind you all day yesterday. By the time he came around, you had already been long gone. No one knew about his church service until later in the day. We had all planned on coming to the wake and funeral regardless. While you were in town, we must have just been leaving the church. When we arrived, there was no car in the driveway and the doors were all locked. We knew you'd be back shortly, so we all have been sitting here, patiently waiting for you. We've got all day, you know."

Huey smiled again. He looked around the crowd aimlessly. "I can't believe Pastor Jones went through all that trouble and arranged that service for him. I'd like to thank him. Where is he?"

Sharon explained, "The pastor disclosed to me that because Elias's animosity was focused on him, he, out of sheer respect for Elias, would not be attending the wake or the funeral. He said that he wanted to abide by Elias's wishes and show him the honor he deserved."

"Wow!" Huey said. "He told you that?"

"Word for word."

"Well," Huey was shocked. "I guess I was wrong about Pastor Jones. Maybe Elias was, too."

"No, you weren't," Sharon chuckled.

"How's that?"

"I said that you weren't wrong about Pastor Jones, and neither was Elias. At the service, he passed around a collection plate. The real reason he stayed behind was to count the money. I saw him pocketing cash as we left the church."

"Really?" Huey smiled at Sharon. "I'll have to see him tomorrow about which worthy cause he's going to donate that collection to, one that Elias would approve of."

Sharon laughed back at Huey. "I knew you'd take care of it." She looked up at the back door. "Do you think it would be possible if we all went inside? All these people are still waiting to see Elias."

Huey looked at the crowd. "Oh right, right." He raised his voice. "Sorry about that, everyone! We can all go inside now." He could hear the approval emerging from the crowd. He squeezed past a few people still sitting on the back steps. "Excuse me, please. Thank you." Unlocking the door, he peeked his head inside, and with a smile on his face, he shouted, "Well Elias, here we come!" Stepping back out, he held the door for each and every person as they entered the house. Holding the screen door with his foot, he shook every hand, patted people on the back, and greeted everyone with a warm, welcoming smile.

People, from all over, brought food of all different kinds. Meats, sides, fruits, desserts, and homemade bread were piled on the kitchen table and counter. It was an amazing display of a buffet. Huey couldn't understand why so many people were bringing food to this wake. He understood the ritual of bringing food to a wake in general. Normally, it is done as an act of kindness to the living family members of the deceased. Dealing with funeral arrangements and being distraught over the loss of a loved one is enough stress to have to overcome without having the added pressure of preparing meals for the family. In this case however, there is no remaining family. Why would all these people go to all this trouble when they know that Elias was the last remaining member of his family?

Huey stopped one of the women entering the house carrying a plate of chicken-fried steak. "Excuse me, Mrs. Cooper. Can I ask you something?"

"Certainly, lad. What would you like to know?" Mrs. Cooper responded.

"Who is all this food for? I mean, Elias is gone, and there is no one left in this house to eat all this."

"Silly boy," she laughed. "Why, it's for you. We all understand how hard it is to plan a funeral. We see what you've gone through the last few days. Elias was a good man, and you were and still are a good friend to him. Over the last year, we haven't treated Elias very well due to our misunderstandings of his displaced anger... but, it's too late to change that now. We decided to do the next best thing. Allow us to show our appreciation for both you and Elias by accepting the gifts we bring. You deserve them as much as Elias or any other family member of his. You were probably as close to family as Elias had the last few years, besides Ellen of course. By doing this, you'll be helping a lot of us make amends and achieve closure with the remorse we feel about our treatment of Elias. Please." Mrs. Cooper handed her plate to Huey.

He smiled at her and accepted the plate warmly. "Thank you, Mrs. Cooper." Huey raised his voice. "Thank you all!"

She continued to look at him, "No, Huey. Thank you."

Over the course of the afternoon, people stayed and talked. They cried and they laughed. Those that were old enough to remember stories of Elias and Ellen from decades ago shared them with the younger generations that never really got to know them. A lot of times, there was silence in the house except for the storyteller. Only Elias could have told these stories better himself. He would have been proud. Proud of Huey. Proud of the whole town. There had never been a bigger gathering in this area for this amount of time over the loss of one person. And there may never be again.

Before it got too dark, Huey went outside and opened the barn. He hooked up the hay wagon to the tractor and threw Elias's riggings up on top of the wagon. He backed the tractor and the wagon up to the back door. Six of the younger men in attendance helped roll Elias on the gurney to the back door, and then they lifted his casket up and onto the hay wagon. With the crowd amassed behind the wagon, they followed Huey as he drove Elias slowly to the back lot where the cemetery was.

Young and old alike walked side by side, still discussing old stories and the man they were there to honor. Everyone that had shown up was still there. No one dared leave now for fear of missing out on something that may never happen again. When these young are old enough, they can tell their children and grandchildren of the day that the town banded together for Elias Morgan.

Huey continued to drive slowly, looking back at all the people, smiling and laughing. He looked at the coffin, bouncing around on the back of the hay wagon. "What a proper and fitting hearse..." he cried "...for a man that worked so hard all of his life, through hard times and sorrow. Huey finally reached the cemetery and circled the tractor around to back it near Elias's grave. Huey had already come back here the night before and dug out Elias's spot next to Ellen while the night air was still cool. It was a last minute decision for him, but it proved to pay off for him today. He hadn't expected this much of a turnout, and if it had come down to it, he was going to just bury him privately. As the situation unfolded today, it would have been a shame and a disservice to Elias and the town if they hadn't closed this perfect afternoon with the proper burial of the man they came to see.

Huey had laid out a green tarp over the freshly dug hole last night. Because of the darkness, he actually dug the hole so wide that he could wipe a small amount of dirt away from the wall and touch Ellen's casket.

As creepy as that may seem, after it had been done, Huey felt pretty good about it. At first, he was a little spooked, but then he thought about how Elias and Ellen would be in constant contact now, both physical and spiritual. It was unintentional, but accidentally romantic.

Before he removed the tarp, he explained to the crowd what had happened, and he described how he now viewed it. He wanted to avoid the shocking gasps before he revealed it. The onlookers seemed to interpret and accept his explanation with good intentions, so Huey removed the tarp with confidence.

After everyone received their opportunity to gape into the hole to see what all the fuss was about, Huey and the six men that helped load Elias onto the hay wagon removed Elias from the main parade float and his final modular voyage. They set Elias down next to the hole and set up the rigging above the grave. Flowers were laid upon the casket, draped across the entire lid. Everyone was given the opportunity to walk by, touch the coffin one last time, and say their own personal peace to Elias. As they all passed by, a low-hummed tune grew from within the line of the marchers. It developed into a louder version of "Amazing Grace", still hummed but distinctly recognizable. Once the seemingly endless line had made its pass, removing individual flower petals as a remembrance of Elias and this day, Huey and the other "pall bearers" rigged the coffin to hover over the empty resting place.

Then, all at once, the humming stopped, and there was complete silence again. The crickets were up and about now, rubbing their legs together all over the place. Everyone was waiting for someone to say some final, memorable, strong, and deserving, etched-in-your-mind-forever words. There was no clergyman

here.   Everyone appeared to be staring at Huey.
Everyone.

Who else had earned this honor? No one. Not one
other man, woman, or child had stood by Elias as a
fellow human being, a brother or sister, or a friend as
Huey had done. No one but Huey even deserved to be
in the presence of this ceremony, this acreage, or these
sacred grounds. But they were. And Huey was the one
that allowed it and made it happen.

If anyone had even uttered one sentence, one phrase,
one word, one sound at that moment in time, it would
have dismantled the meaning behind everything that
transpired there that day.   Huey was the only
acceptable speaker at that exact moment. And he knew
it. But he wanted to make sure that they knew it. He
scanned the faces and eyes of the nearby onlookers
through the darkness. He saw and felt, even in the pitch
black sky, the approval in the eyes of the unworthy. He
was nervous about what to say. He didn't want to fail,
to let anyone down, to let Elias down. But he couldn't
fail. He knew that, too. He knew, from the time he
walked into this house Monday morning, what he was
going to say in this final moment. Whether it was too
many or voiced alone, it was the same thing. Now was
the time to speak. He closed his eyes, opened his mind
and mouth, and in the darkness...he spoke.

"Here lies the body of a man. Nothing more, nothing less. He worked hard from the time he could walk to the time he could not. All of his scars, both internal and external, were earned, but well hidden. He lived a life as every man should, failing no one, but himself and God. He was a good man that did good things, but was unrecognized for it. His struggles were taken in stride, but they left damage that no man should have to endure. He lost both a wife and a child before he succumbed to God's will. Today, this one man has achieved something no single person here ever will. He brought a town together as one. He was a good friend. I will miss him dearly. And today, whether remembered by many or remembered by one, he will still be remembered. Here lies the body of Elias Morgan."

With those final words, silence returned. Even the crickets stopped chirping as they lowered Elias into his rightful place next to Ellen. Huey grabbed the nearby shovel and sifted one light layer of dirt over his casket. The crowd then dispersed, never uttering one noise until they were back at their cars. And in that instant, they filed out as they had filed in...as a unit, single and undivided. As the final taillight turned from the driveway, Huey was left alone by the grave of his honored friend. He took one last look in the darkness, got on the tractor, and pulled away to the barn. He locked up the equipment in the barn, locked up the back door to the house, and got into his car, which was now full of delicious smelling food that someone had politely placed on his back seat for him. He was going to go home and eat, because he hadn't eaten since breakfast. Then, it was straight to bed for him. It had been a long, draining day, but it was a good day. And tonight, he would sleep like a baby.

CHAPTER 18

Huey woke the next morning with a smile on his face. He did in fact sleep like a baby. It was a deep, continuous sleep. He woke refreshed and ready to finish the job from last night. He threw on the same dirty clothes that he wore to dig the hole, grabbed some toast, and headed out of his home.

It was quite early in the morning. The sun was just now completely in view over the horizon. The previous night's air was just starting to warm. By noon, it would be a blistering heat. Right now was a good time to fill in a grave. Huey got in his car and drove over to Ridgeway farm. He pulled in the driveway and parked back by the barn door. Opening the barn, he unhitched the tractor from the hay wagon, grabbed a square-tip shovel and a hoe, and hopped onto the tractor. It made no sense to break a sweat just walking to the cemetery when he could drive the tractor out there. Save the sweat for the actual labor. He started the tractor and pulled out of the barn, heading for the cemetery. It was a nice, slow, scenic drive out there, but he did have to hurry. The sheriff was still on his week's vacation, so he was still in charge of taking care of all the police business. When he finally reached the back lot, he shut off the tractor and hopped off, tools in hand.

Everything was as Huey left it last night. Huey was afraid to leave things as they were, but it was late... and extremely dark. He was relieved to see that no one had come back there in between now and then. He probably should have pulled the tarp over the hole, but it didn't seem to matter now.

Huey looked down into the grave. Nothing had fallen down in there, and nothing was changed. It was all still there...the gleaming metal casket, the layer of flowers, and the thin layer of dirt. "Good," Huey thought.

Now, it was time to get to work. He folded up the green tarp and placed it on the back of the tractor, so he wouldn't forget it. Grabbing the square shovel, he began scooping shovelfuls of dirt into the hole. This was the easy part. Digging the hole was torture on his hands and back. This was just scoop and toss, scoop and toss. It was monotonous though, so it was still very tiring. To break up the rhythm every now and then, Huey would drop the shovel, grab the hoe, and just push the dirt into the hole. Pretty soon, the shovel was retired, and the hoe was all that he was using.

Two hours had flown by since he had started, and Huey was just about done. The mound of dirt, which sat two feet away at dawn, was now back in its original location. The ground was still a small hill from a lack of settlement, but Huey could take care of that some other day. He wanted to smack it down a little with the square-nosed shovel, and then, call it a day to attend to his official duties. He picked up the shovel and went to lift the blade above his head so that it was parallel to the ground. As he raised it, he noticed something on the bottom of the blade that he hadn't noticed before. There appeared to be something there, but he wasn't sure. He rotated the shovel to examine it and lifted off his sunglasses. There were two small spots of a dark red color that seem to be dried onto the blade. He drew the blade in closer to his face and in that instant, he heard a faint voice, shouting.

Scared half to death, he dropped the shovel and looked up to see a shadow of a figure approaching him from the direction of the farmhouse. Between the sweat in his eyes and the humidity in the air, he couldn't quite make out who it was until they got a lot closer. The combination of manual labor and being startled exhausted Huey greatly, though, and he barely had the strength to fight. He picked up the shovel but still took a seat on the tire of the tractor with his hands tightly gripping the long, wooden handle. Wiping the sweat from his brow with his sleeve, he waited until the silhouette came into focus. Once he could distinguish a face, he dropped the shovel from his grip and removed the handkerchief from his shirt pocket, wiped off his hands, then wiped the sweat from his eyes and replaced it in his shirt pocket.

It was Attorney Woodward. Huey extended his hand to the lawyer and spoke, "Hollis, how are you?"

"Good morning, Huey. I thought I might find you out here. I was shouting out your name, but I guess you couldn't hear me."

Huey chuckled, "Oh, I heard you...very faintly...but I heard you. You startled me. I almost thought you were Elias calling out to me from that hole over there."

"Sorry about that. Is that the old son-of-a-gun underneath all that fresh dirt over there?" He pointed to Elias's grave.

Huey replied, "Yes, sir. I just finished filling him in."

"I'm gonna miss that old goat."

"As will I, Hollis. As will I."

"Hey Huey, if you got a minute, I'd like to discuss a few things with you."

"Well Hollis, if you don't mind, could we do this back at the farmhouse? I'm pretty much done here, and I need to get back to my job. I drove my squad car here with a clean uniform in the trunk. I just have to pick up these tools and I'll give you a ride back on the tractor. We can discuss things over a nice, cold glass of water. Then, I'm sure Elias wouldn't mind if I used his shower to freshen up. Does that sound alright?"

"That'll be just fine."

Huey picked up the shovel and hoe and headed back to the tractor. He turned to Hollis. "You don't mind holdin' some stuff, do you?"

"Not at all. I'd be happy to help."

Huey allowed Hollis to climb onto the back of the tractor first. He handed him the tarp, shovel, and hoe before hopping into the driver's seat and starting the tractor. As they pulled away back towards the house, Hollis scanned the scenery from the rear point-of-view.

"Haven't ever been back here before. It sure is beautiful," Hollis said.

"It sure is," Huey agreed. "It sure is."

When they got back to the driveway, Huey pulled straight into the barn and turned off the tractor. Hollis hopped off first and Huey followed suit.

"Where do these go?" Hollis asked, holding up the tools.

"Just lay them down over there, Hollis. I'll put them away later. Thanks."

"No problem." Hollis looked around the barn, sniffing and making a nasty face. "Do you smell something? It smells awful in here, like something crawled up and died...Do you smell that?"

Huey laughed. "Hollis, you're a city boy. Everything out on the farm smells like something died to you. Elias has probably got some manure lying around here somewhere. I'm so used to farm life. I don't notice anything anymore. Let's get you in the house before you throw up."

Hollis nodded in agreement while holding his nose. In a nasally voice, he replied, "Yes. Let's go...Hurry!"

Both men left the barn and Huey locked the door behind them. "Let me go get my uniform out of the trunk first," said Huey. "Alright then," said Hollis. They both walked to the squad car. Huey opened the trunk, took out his uniform, and closed the trunk again. They walked to the house, and Huey held the back door open for Hollis. "Take a seat in the kitchen, and I'll get us some water."

"Thank you," replied Hollis.

Huey opened the cabinets to get some glasses while Hollis took a seat. He removed a glass pitcher of water from the fridge and filled each glass. Handing a glass to Hollis, he spoke.

"I missed you at the funeral yesterday. Were you there at all?"

"No, Huey, but that's kind of why I'm here today."

"I don't understand."

"After you left my office on Monday, my interest in Elias's estate was piqued. You saw how my office was that day, right?"

"You mean papers all over the place and stacked three feet high?" replied Huey.

"Exactly. I lifted every paper in every stack and couldn't find anything. I knew that I had something on Elias, but I couldn't remember what. I searched for three days. With every stack I finished unsuccessful, my curiosity grew tenfold. I wasn't about to go home until I found it. I slept in the office. I hadn't changed my clothes or showered since Monday."

"Really?"

"Yeah. But last night, I slept in my own bed. I showered this morning and I changed my clothes."

Huey questioned, "Does that mean you found something?"

"Indeed, I did. The last place I looked last night should have been my first. About six months ago, I stopped using my file cabinet. It was full and I was going to get a new one, but I never got around to it. I started stacking papers then. Last night, I sat in the chair at my desk and unintentionally stared right at the damn cabinet. And then, it hit me to look in there. The file cabinet was organized chronologically, and the very last file that I put in there was labeled ELIAS MORGAN. It was one of those smack-myself-in-the-head stupidity moments.

Huey was excited. "So... what was in the folder?"

"Two things."

"Do you have them with you, Hollis?"

"Right here." He handed over two letter-sized envelopes. One was sealed. The other was not.

"Wait a minute… should I be reading these? Is this legal, Hollis?"

"Legal and binding. You won't get in any trouble either, Huey."

"Why's that?"

"They're addressed to you."

Huey gave Hollis a confused smile as he opened up the unsealed envelope and began reading. Hollis continued talking while he read.

"According to Elias's instructions, I was to give you both of these envelopes upon his death. I was instructed to leave the sealed one intact as your eyes were the only to fall upon its contents. The unsealed envelope is a will that Elias had me draw up while he was still of sound mind."

"Is all of this correct?" Huey asked.

"It most certainly is. That will declares you, Huey Scott, as the sole heir of Elias's Ridgeway Farm estate. It includes any and all buildings and property located within the grounds. Every inch of every acre is yours, at your disposal, to do with what you may."

Huey was stunned. "Are you sure? There's no one else?"

"There are no living heirs in the Ridgeway or Morgan family. This will need not go to probate because there is no one to legally contest it. Elias never had the need to take out loans for anything. Elias assured me that there are no liens out against anything that he owns. Everything is yours, free and clear. He told me that the sealed envelope would explain it all. If you need help understanding any of this or if anyone gives you any trouble, please feel free to call me and I will help you take care of it."

"Wow...I'm speechless...I...I just can't believe it."

"He told me how much he thought you deserved it, and I agree with him." Hollis got up from his chair. "Well, I will leave you to your letter. I have a lot of work to catch up on. I'm on my way now to find a second file cabinet. I think it's about time, don't you?"

"Yeah...Yeah." Huey kept staring at that sealed envelope.

Hollis realized that Huey probably didn't even hear the last thing he said. He laughed out loud. "You have a good afternoon, Huey. Take care and try to get some work done. Once again, call me if you need me."

"Yeah... Yeah." Huey was definitely in a trance.

Hollis yelled, "Hey, Huey!!"

Startled, Huey shook his head and looked at Hollis.

Hollis quieted down and smiled. "Don't worry about using the shower in this house... It's yours now." He closed the back screen door behind him as he exited, leaving Huey standing in the kitchen, still holding the sealed envelope.

CHAPTER 19

Huey heard Hollis start his car and pull out of the driveway. Immediately, he grabbed a knife from the silverware drawer, slitting open the envelope and removing the letter. He opened it up and began reading it aloud as he sat in the kitchen chair without looking.

Huey, I know Hollis has just explained the easy part to you. The easy part is that I have left Ridgeway Farm and all that goes with it to you. You have been a good and loyal friend. You are hard-working, and I know that I have left my life's blood in good hands. Hopefully, you will accept this with open arms and treat this gift as a reward for all of the selfless acts you have demonstrated over the years for Ellen and me. And right now, I'm sure that this is all a lot to absorb, but it is not the end. There is a much harder part that I hope you can accept and forgive me for. Actually, you're going to have to forgive a lot of people after I fill you in…So, I guess I'll just come out and tell you.

The hard part that I need to tell you is that there is another reason why I am leaving you this farm. Not that you don't deserve it, because you do. However, it is the same reason why I've always treated you as family all these years. It is because you are family.

Huey, you are my nephew. Your father, Josiah Scott and I are brothers...and you are the true blood-born heir of this farm. You are the only one left. You did have another uncle named Leroy Turner. He did marry, but he never had any children and now he and his spouse have long passed.

I know this all may be confusing, but please let me explain. Your grandfather, my pa, was a mean-spirited, selfish person who never treated our ma or us boys with any respect. He would constantly argue with Ma and he would beat us boys. He was a traveling salesman, so whenever he left town, we would all be relieved until he came back. At any point, we probably could have picked up and moved while he was gone, but we couldn't afford to go anywhere, so we stayed. Besides, this farm belonged to Ma. It was her family's farm, the Ridgeways, and it had been free and clear for at least two hundred years.

Eventually, we started to notice that Pa was leaving town with no luggage and nothing to sell. We soon discovered that he was no longer traveling very far. He was just going into town, staying for a few days, and then returning; sometimes with money and sometimes not. Your father, Josiah, stealthily followed him into town one day, only to spot him cavorting around town with a well-to-do single woman. When Josiah returned to inform Ma, it seemed as if she had already known. It only went on for a little while longer before Pa finally left us for good. I hadn't even reached double digits in age yet.

My pa left us for that other woman. He had been charming her into paying him for escorting her places, showing her a good time, and eventually sharing intimate time with her. Pa was not an ugly man. He could have just about wooed any woman in that town, but he was as hooked on this woman as she was on him. And we were all on the line about it. In one aspect, we were losing a father and a source of income, when there was some. On the other hand, we were losing all the bickering, the yelling, the beatings, and the other abuse that he always brought home with him.

Though it was hard while he was still there, it got much harder after he left. Ma became ill and we all had to grow up real fast. There came a point when our mother could no longer help us. She was stuck in bed and could not muster the strength to help with the day-to-day chores around the house. When all the chores had been done for the day, we would sit around the bed and listen to her read to us from her favorite book, a collection of short stories from Edgar Allen Poe. She had read it as a child and fell in love with it. She was rather upset about not being able to help, so to help us relax after a tolling day, she felt compelled to share with us something that she truly cherished. It gave purpose to her day to see us withdrawn into the stories. I still have her copy of the

184

book on the shelf in the living room, if you'd like to look at it.

Huey stopped reading and smiled. "Dad used to read to me from the same book." He continued reading the letter aloud.

Pa had a clingy personality, however, and we all knew he wouldn't be gone long without resurfacing.

And he did. He would come up with all kinds of excuses: he needed his clothes, he wanted his half of the farm, and he missed us. We grew extremely weary of it. At some point, my brothers decided that I was old enough to take care of Ma on my own. When they were old enough, they each moved out.

Afraid that he would follow them, each of my brothers changed their name, dropping the Morgan, and used their middle names as their new last names. Your father was Josiah Scott Morgan, and our other brother was Leroy Turner Morgan. Josiah Scott and Leroy Turner each moved to different cities, far enough away that Pa could not find them. I originally had some minimal contact with both of them over the years, but that dwindled down eventually to nothing as we grew much older. They attended my wedding, but I did not attend theirs, out of respect for their new-found anonymity in their new communities. Everyone around here knew who they were, but no one where they lived knew who I was.

I knew of your birth as well. Leroy's wife could not have children. When you came to town a few years back looking for a job, I knew who you were from the minute you entered the city limits. If I had said something then, it would have stirred up a lot more trouble than it is right now.

If you're looking to substantiate all of this story, go into the living room and look on the bookshelf. In between Ellen's personal Bible and Ma's Edgar Allen Poe book is a very old book. This is the Ridgeway Family Bible. From the immigrants leaving England to the current, every Ridgeway's vitals are in that book, including your father. It is a sacred book to our family, so please treat it well.

Huey stopped reading again. "Could've used that insight a few days ago. Would've saved a lot of time. Oh well. The search and discovery made it so much more exciting and important to me anyway." He continued reading the letter.

Sorry to digress, but back to me and my ma. After Josiah and Leroy left, I was the only one to retain the Morgan name. Ma's name was listed as Morgan on all the property deeds by then. It would have been too much

186

of a hassle to change it all back over to Ridgeway. Believe me; I would have tossed out that man's name a long time ago too, if it wasn't for the farm. I was put on the deed with no issues, and then, Ma got really sick. Near the end of her life, I had to neglect the farm to cater to her constant needs. I also spent some time going into town to keep tabs on my pa. I wanted to be prepared in case he was planning on returning to the farm. He never did return to Ridgeway Farm. The woman he left Ma for ended up marrying him, and she was more controlling than he was. It makes me smile, even today, to think about him getting the same treatment that he gave us. Once I realized that, I stopped spying on him.

Soon after that, Ma passed away, and I was left alone on the farm. Disgusted with the way the farm looked, I decided to fix the place back up to what it used to look like. I would work on it most of the day, go into town in late afternoon, and eat at the diner for supper. To make money for food, I would do odd jobs around town, mostly on weekends. I really ate only one decent meal a day, and that was at the diner.

And that is where I met Ellen. We would share a soda, finish a crossword puzzle together, and converse all night. It wasn't long before we were married. You already know most of the stories about Ellen and me, though. I know that I've told them to you many times over. I haven't told you too much about our daughter,

187

Sarah, though. Sarah was born while we were still in our mid-twenties. She grew up on this farm faster than we realized. We loved her very much as I know that she loved us. Because of ma's need for me on the farm, I had barely pushed through high school, and I was determined to not let that happen to Sarah. Ellen and I both made sure that she went into town to attend school and get a decent education. Parents always want better for their children you know? Before long, Sarah had grown and had graduated from high school. She had always been a beautiful, little girl in my eyes, but she had grown intellectually as well. It had always been my intentions to push Sarah to make something of her life and to travel away from this farm. She could have been anything that she set her mind on, but my darling, little girl didn't want to leave this calm, serene life. She didn't want the hustle and bustle of a big city. All she really wanted was to settle down and have a family like her parents did in this small town. Instead of going off to college in some crowded town, she stayed at home on the farm. She got a job in town as a teller at the bank. Sarah did well enough with her job to help us pay for our bills at home when we struggled. Eventually, she fell in love with a man, and we were happy for her. We never actually met him, but she would go into town on the weekends to see him. She was deeply in love with him, but he must not have felt the same way about her. He broke it off with her after just six months, leaving her extremely depressed. It was evident to Ellen and me that Sarah was not getting past this relationship. We tried to console her, but she just wasn't accepting it. At the young age of thirty, our beloved Sarah could not take the pain anymore, and she ended her own life. We were never the same after that.

Well, Huey, that should just about catch you up on everything. I hope I've answered a lot of questions for you, and I hope that you can forgive me for not telling you sooner. I was just trying to honor your father's wishes until my last breath. All these years, I treated you as my nephew anyway. I think deep down you felt like family in this house whether you knew or not.

Do what you will with this farm, but please respect that this has belonged to our family for over two hundred years. I know that you will make me proud no matter what you do. I guess that is it. Ellen and I love you Huey. Always remember that…and maybe we'll see each other again someday.

Uncle Elias.

Huey put down the letter, unable to speak. His chest was hurting, but it was extremely warm. He sat for another minute before getting up to look around the house. The whole house looked differently to him now. Nothing had changed but the ownership of all that sat

189

around him. He stepped out the back door into the back yard, walking slowly and taking in everything with a different set of eyes now. He opened up the barn door and looked in at his new inventory. All these old tools... his. The tractor and trailer... his. The truck... his.

Huey stopped. "Wait a minute," he said. He thought back to the day that he pulled Elias over. When Huey had asked Elias about the truck, Elias told him that the truck belonged to his brother. Huey was confused. "Dad never owned a truck. I don't know if my new uncle Leroy ever did, but maybe I should check that out. I'll go run the VIN at the office... The office."

CHAPTER 20

Huey had completely forgotten all about going into work. He had better go in and get ready before the whole day was shot. He pulled a pen from his pocket and walked over to the truck. After writing the VIN on his hand, he shut and locked the barn door. Going inside, he rewrote the number from his hand onto a scrap piece of paper. He grabbed his uniform from the kitchen counter and ran upstairs to get ready. After a quick shower and a brushing of his teeth, Huey got dressed and ran downstairs and out the door, to his squad car. He started the car and shifted into gear in one, smooth motion. Pulling onto the highway, he sped into town.

Arriving at the station, he parked the car and got out. As he approached the door, he noticed something in front of it, on the steps. There were several bouquets of flowers and planters sitting there, each with a personal note attached. They were all for him. Everyone had a personal attachment to the service for Elias yesterday, and they wanted to show Huey just how much they appreciated all that he did to help them experience that. He unlocked the door and propped it open to slide all the presents inside the office. They would definitely help to beautify the station. Once the flowers were all inside, he closed the door.

Huey walked over to the desk with the answering machine on it and pressed the button to play the messages recorded on the tape. Turning up the volume on the machine, he walked over to his own desk and sat down. None of the messages appeared to be emergencies, so he could make his rounds attending to them later. The one thing that kept pressing on his mind was the truck in the barn. He picked up the phone on his desk and started dialing. Reaching into his shirt pocket, he pulled out the slip of paper with the Vehicle Identification Number on it. The phone rang and rang and rang. Finally, someone on the other end picked up. It was a female voice that sounded through the receiver, "Tennessee state police. How may I help you?"

"Hello. This is Sheriff's Deputy Huey... " He paused, looking off into the distance and smiling. He continued, " ...Morgan... " This was the first time he used that name, and it showed a commitment to changing his name back to his original heritage. He was honored to do it, and it made him feel warm inside to say it aloud... but in that moment he realized that he probably shouldn't use it in official business until it was legalized. "... no, wait... Huey Scott... yes, Scott... from the Fellowship office. I would like to request a VIN lookup for a vehicle, please."

The voice on the other end replied, "Please hold while I transfer your call to the Motor Vehicle Division." Again, the phone rang and rang. Eventually, a male voice answered the call, "Motor Vehicles."

"Good afternoon. This is Deputy Huey Morgan from Fellowship. I have a vehicle that I need information on."

"Do you have a VIN, sir?"

"Yes, I do. It's...," Huey rattled off the number and waited. He could hear file cabinet drawers opening and the sound of fingers walking through folders and papers in the background. A drawer would slam shut and another would open. Then, there was silence as the person searching scanned the paper in front of him. Silence was again broken as the searcher discovered what he was looking for.

"Ah. Here it is." The motor vehicle department worker read off the information for the vehicle to Huey, but something was not right. Huey was puzzled. "Could you repeat that, sir? I want to be sure that I have the right information."

"Certainly, officer." The employee read the information aloud again for Huey.

"Thank you. One more thing. Are there license plates registered to that particular vehicle?"

"I'll have to check. That information is in a different location, sir. One moment please." The worker set down the phone, and Huey heard more file cabinet drawers opening and slamming shut. There was a lot more rustling of papers before the staff member picked the phone back up and started talking again. "Officer, I found the information you are looking for. Here is the plate registered to that vehicle." He read the plate number and who the plate was registered to back to Huey.

"Thank you, sir," Huey said. "You have been a great help to me. I really appreciate it."

"You're quite welcome. It was a break from this monotonous job to do that for you. I should be thanking you. If you need anything else, please feel free to call back and I will be more than happy to take another break for you. You have a nice day now."

"You, too. Thanks again." Huey hung up the phone. He looked at the notes that he had jotted down during the call. Some things matched, and some things didn't. The vehicle in the barn is the same year, make, and model as the vehicle on the paper. The vehicle and the license plate are registered to the same man, and he has been the only known owner of this truck. The owner is not Elias and does not have the last names, Scott or Morgan. Also, the truck is a different color now than the registered vehicle.

Huey was so intrigued by all this new information that he couldn't stop searching for the truth... but he would have to postpone it for now. He can't ignore his work commitments any longer. Folding up the paper with the truck info on it, Huey stuffed it into his uniform shirt pocket. He got up from his desk and walked over to the desk with the answering machine on it. He pressed play again to listen to the messages. The first time, he hadn't really paid attention. His mind was stuck on that truck. As the tape was replayed, he paid closer attention this time and actually wrote down the complaints and concerns that he was hearing in the background behind him.

When the tape was done, he stopped it and grabbed his coat before locking the station door on his way out. There were five courtesy calls he had to pay before he could go home this evening. His personal investigation would have to wait until tomorrow or the weekend. As long as he left right now, Huey could probably finish by suppertime. They were all simple, solvable problems and Huey could definitely handle it with reasonable quickness and fairness. He hopped into the squad car and headed towards his first destination.

CHAPTER 21

The next morning was Friday, and Huey was up bright and early. He was fed, bathed, clothed, and at the station by eight o'clock. He had finished all of yesterday's calls before supper as he had expected and now his morning was open until someone called. Huey figured he could stay at the office until noon, waiting for calls. Then, he could go get some lunch and re-start his search for the truck owner.

By the time the clock struck, Huey still hadn't received one call. He grabbed his coat from the back of the chair and locked the station door behind him. Trotting over to the squad car, he got in and drove over to the diner to grab a quick bite to eat. He parked the car and got out to head into the diner. Upon entering the diner, he approached the counter looking for the waitress, Sharon. Sharon had been back in the kitchen. She finally emerged and spotted Huey.

"Hey, Huey! How are ya? You gonna sit down today and have some lunch?"

"Not today, Sharon," he said. "I'm on a mission today and I don't have the time. Would you mind just whipping up an egg-salad sandwich for me... and a side of coleslaw?"

"Sure thing, honey. I see you're in a hurry, so I'll do it myself. Be right back." Sharon went back into the kitchen and within two minutes, emerged with a paper sack filled with Huey's order. As she handed the bag over to him, she inquired, "So, you're on a mission today. Where you headin'?"

"I'm on my way to find out about a truck that's been spotted in the area. It's kind of hush-hush, though. Can't really talk about it."

Sharon smiled and winked at him, "Gotcha. I won't say a thing."

"How much do I owe you for the food?"

She smiled again and said, "You know what? You're on a mission. Can't be worrying about money and all. Lunch is on the house, Huey. Hopefully, that'll brighten up your day."

"Thank you, Sharon. I appreciate that. Got a lot on my mind right now."

"You just remember that when I call you tomorrow to take me to the show," she laughed.

Huey blushed. He wasn't used to that kind of attention. "It's a date. Call me tomorrow morning at the station, alright?" He held up the bag to wave as he hurried out the door. "Thanks again!"

Sharon waved back, giggling and cradling a menu to her chest with the other hand. "See you tomorrow!"

Huey got in the car and sped off. What just happened kind of startled him a bit... but it was a good thing. He always had a little crush on Sharon but never had the guts to say or do anything about it. Keeping his eyes on the road, he reached into the sack on the passenger seat for the sandwich. He pulled it out and opened it from the cellophane wrapped around it. She had cut off the crust and carved it into the shape of a heart. He blushed again and took a big bite out of it. That was probably the best egg-salad sandwich he ever had. He would have to thank her again tomorrow.

Once he finished the sandwich, Huey's concentration returned to the task at hand. His first destination was in town. He headed over to 403 Cypress Road. It was the home of Mrs. Clara Glisson, a widow of forty years. It was also the last known residence of the truck owner. As soon as Huey saw the address during his phone conversation, he recognized it. He needed some clues, and maybe he could get some answers from Clara. Or, maybe he would find the truck owner.

Huey pulled into the driveway of the Glisson home. There were no vehicles in the driveway, but that wasn't peculiar. Clara hadn't driven for at least twenty years. Her husband's car was probably still under a tarp in the garage, collecting dust. More than likely, Clara was home. Huey got out of the squad car and walked over to the steps of the front porch. With his hands on his hips, he gave the wooden, forest-green, one-story home a once over. The home was broken down, but it seemed to be in some mode of repair. The eave had some new boards on it that didn't match the rest of the house. Whoever replaced them must not have been able to find the exact same shade of green to duplicate the rest of the boards. Regardless, they had been replaced during the last six months. Half of the window shutters had been restored as well. Clara must have hired someone to do all this work.

Huey ascended the steps on the front porch and noticed one of the front window curtains move. Someone was home. He opened the screen door and began knocking on the front door. Before he could get in the second knock, the door flew open and a small-framed elderly woman stood before him. She was dressed in a nightgown and her hair was in curlers. Her eyes were magnified through the thick lenses in her glasses. It was Mrs. Clara Glisson.

"Well, well... If it isn't Huey Scott! Let me look at you. Well, don't just stand there. Come on in," she said without pausing. She turned and headed back inside her home. Huey followed her inside.

"It's Huey Morgan now," said Huey.

"What's that?" she interrupted, yelling loudly. Clara was hard of hearing and she was facing the other way. Besides, the television was on, and it as blaring. "I'm sorry, but I couldn't hear you, Huey."

Huey smiled and leaned over closer to her. "I'm going to turn this television volume down, so we can talk." He reached over and turned down the volume gradually.

"Not too low, son. My stories are on," Clara said, as she sat down in her chair.

Huey smiled again. "What I was saying before was that my name is Huey Morgan. I've recently discovered that my father's last name was originally Morgan, so I've decided to change my name back to that."

"Is that any relation to Elias Morgan?"

"Yes, ma'am. He's my uncle... my father's brother," Huey replied.

"Did you come over here just to tell me that? You know, my stories are on."

Huey laughed out loud. "No, ma'am. I have a few questions to ask you, if you don't mind?"

"Personal questions, or police questions?" Clara asked.

"I guess you can say that they're a bit of both... "

"'Cause you know my stories are on," she interrupted.

"Yes, ma'am. I won't make this long. Is that alright?"

"Certainly, Mr. Huey <u>Morgan</u>. What are you waiting on?"

He chuckled again and reached unto his uniform shirt pocket. He pulled out the folded-up sheet of paper from the phone call, unfolded it, and handed it to her. "Mrs. Glisson, do you recognize the name on this sheet of paper?"

She squinted at the paper. "Having trouble seeing this. Let me get my reading glasses." She got up and headed towards the dining room.

"What glasses do you have on? Let me guess. Your st..."

"Story-watching glasses!" Clara yelled out, finishing his words.

"I could have read it to you."

"Nonsense," Clara responded. "A woman my age has got to do things for herself. It helps to keep me sharp, you know?" She returned from the dining room with her reading glasses and sat back down in the chair. Taking off the glasses she had on, she positioned her reading glasses on the tip of her nose. Her new glasses magnified her eyes even more, making her head look that much smaller. She picked up the paper that Huey originally handed to her and started reading. "Oh sure, I know him."

"You do?" Huey's spirits lifted as he heard her say that. He was certain that this was going to be a dead-end, but he had to try.

"Yes, sir. He's been renting a room here from me for about a year now," said Clara.

"He has?"

"That's what I said. You hard-of-hearing, too?" She handed him back the paper.

"No, ma'am. I'm just surprised to hear that. I thought I knew everyone in this town," Huey responded.

"Well, I guess you know everyone... minus one. Such a nice man, too. He came to town about a year ago, and he's been living here since day one. Is he in trouble?"

"Do you know where he is right now?" Huey asked.

"That depends on if he's in trouble."

"I'll take that as a yes, then."

Mrs. Glisson snapped back, "No. I don't know where he's at right now! He hasn't set foot in this house for almost three weeks now. I've been rather worried. It's not like him to not come home every night."

"If you're worried about home, then why didn't you call the station?"

"He's a grown man. I'm not his ma, and I'm not his wife. It's none of my business," she said.

"Do you think he ran off because he owes you rent?"

"Not in the least. I barely ask for any money. He can't afford it right now and he knows I won't throw him out. He's been helping to fix up the place as partial payment. I get by fairly well on my dear Harold's pension, so I'd rather have him fixing this old place. He's a contractor, you know?"

"A contractor, you say?"

Clara acknowledged, "Yeah. He's got a nice truck that he works out of. Does lots of odd jobs. He's been working with a lot of cinderblock lately. I've been doing his laundry for him. There's dust in everything."

"Really? You say he came to town a year ago. Did he ever mention why?"

"He talked a lot about looking up an old friend."

"An old friend?" Huey questioned.

"Yep. The way he talked about this friend, I don't think it was a man either. Do you get my drift?" she said.

"Why would you think that?"

"I've watched enough stories to know what people are thinking. I could tell by his tone of voice and mannerisms. You know, when he talked about his friend, he kept looking up and smiling. I'm a good people-reader."

Huey looked down at the notes that he had been jotting down while talking. "So, let me get this straight. He's been here a year, looking for a friend who is probably female, is a contractor with a truck, and has been missing for a month."

"That is correct," Clara answered.

"Is there anything else that I should know? How would I recognize him?"

"He'd be the one person in town that you don't know."

"Seriously," said Huey

"I don't know. He's normal looking. He has black hair. Oh...and he always wears the same overalls. You never know what he's going to be working on."

"Overalls. Got it." Huey got up from his chair. "Do you mind if I take a look around his room, Mrs. Glisson? I'll only be a minute."

"Sure, Huey. I'll show you where it is." Clara got up from her chair. "Not much in there, though. He didn't have a lot of baggage when he got here."

Huey followed her, mumbling under his breath. "That's for me to decide."

Clara led him down the hallway, in through the kitchen, and into a back bedroom. It was very small with only one small window. Huey turned to Clara. "If you'd like to go sit back down and rest while I look around, I think I can manage from here on out."

"That's fine, but please don't mess through his stuff too much. If he comes back home and finds that his personals have been rifled through, then he might get angry with me."

"Rest assured, Mrs. Glisson. It is my job to search through rooms with the least amount of disturbance."

"All right then, Huey. I'll leave you be." Clara turned and walked away, leaving Huey alone in the room. Huey turned and right away started opening dresser drawers. The bottom two were completely empty. Clara was right about one thing. He didn't have a lot of stuff. The upper drawers had enough clothes in them for about a week. There were only a few papers in the very top drawer, but they were mostly gas receipts. He moved to the closet. Sliding open the closet door, there were a lot of empty hangers. Only one hanger was being used to hold some folded up overalls. "This must be his spare pair," Huey thought. There was a lone hat box up on the closet shelf. Huey reached for it to check the contents.

As he slid the hatbox off the shelf, an envelope fell to the floor at his feet. He opened the hatbox while it was still in his hands. The box was empty, but he noticed the hat size before returning it to the shelf: 7 ¾. "Wow," Huey thought. "Big head." Huey picked up the envelope. It was sealed. He looked at the front of it. There was no address or postmark. It must have been hand-delivered or left for him. There were two things written on the envelope: the name on Huey's sheet and what Huey read aloud. "Love, your little Junebug."

Huey placed the envelope back underneath the hatbox on the shelf. The envelope was old and yellowed from age. It had been in this man's possession for a long time... and it was still sealed for a reason. Although Huey had permission from Clara to search the room, he didn't want to renege on his promise to her to not disturb too much. This letter hadn't gone through the mail service, so it wouldn't be a federal offense to open it. However, if this guy does come back and finds his letter open, then Clara would have a lot of explaining to do. Huey didn't want to cause trouble for Clara. Huey closed the closet door and dresser drawers and returned to the main living room, retracing his path to Clara.

"Well, if I have any more questions, I'll be back, Mrs. Glisson. I'll leave you to your stories again."

"Damn near over now. There's another one starting though."

"Thank you so much for all your help. I'll be going now."

"Could you turn the volume back up? I have to find my story watching glasses."

"They're in your lap, Mrs. Glisson."

"So they are. You don't mind lettin' yourself out, do you Huey?"

"Not at all." He noticed that she wasn't even listening to him anymore. He opened the front door, walked out to the porch, and shut the door behind him. He gave the neighborhood a once-over from the porch before stepping down and walking to the car.

It was now mid-afternoon. He wasn't long in the Glisson house, but he got a lot of answers. Maybe he should go back to the farm, cook himself an early supper, and think about what he learned today? After all, it was his farm now. It was sort of late to do anymore investigating today, because he had to evaluate all that he just learned and had no idea which direction to go... yet. He got in his car and headed back to the farm, but he needed to stop and get some groceries before he got there. On the way, he thought about how many pieces of the puzzle that Mrs. Glisson filled in and where he was going to go tomorrow.

CHAPTER 22

Huey got up on Saturday morning, and he went through his regular "Saturday morning routine". Before he left the farm, he walked along the side of the house to Ellen's garden. He picked two of the longest-stem roses from the bunch, and using his pocket knife, he cut the flowers at their base. Going back in the house, he cut them again under some running water at the sink and put them in a vase for later. Then, he left the house and farm. Driving his squad car over to his old place, he grabbed a nice outfit to wear later out of his closet. He laid it nice and flat on the back seat of the car, and then, Huey proceeded over to the station. He went inside and checked his messages before sitting down at his desk. There was nothing.

Saturday mornings in Fellowship were usually slow. Most full-time workers spent their days off cutting the grass. Stores in town opened much later than during the week. Anyone that was out partying on Friday night was at home, sleeping off a hangover. Huey loved the quietness on Saturday mornings. As of right then, he only had minimal... tedious... draining paperwork to do that involved his employment as a deputy.

He sat there, working on unfinished paperwork, for about an hour, though it seemed much longer, before the phone rang. He answered it. "Fellowship Sheriff's office. Deputy Huey Morgan speaking. How may I help you?"

A soft, feminine voice spoke on the other end. "Huey Morgan, huh? That has a nice ring to it. Is that something new you're trying?" It was Sharon.

Immediately, Huey's voice changed. He didn't know why, but it did. He spoke much deeper now. "Sharon, I've been expect... I mean... I've been wait... I mean... So nice of you to call. How can I help you?"

"It hasn't been twenty-four hours, and you've already forgotten."

"Forgotten what?" Huey asked.

"About our date today. You're supposed to take me to the show, right? You told me to call you at the station in the morning." Sharon didn't sound angry, just disappointed.

"I didn't forget our date. I just forgot that I told you to call me in the morning. I've had a rough week, you know."

"Oh, I'm sorry. I forgot about the funeral and all." Sharon's voice seemed to perk up.

"See. We all forget things. I was thinking that instead of going to the show, that I could cook you some supper."

"Isn't your place a little small to cook supper?"

"I was thinking of the farmhouse at Ridgeway Farms. There's a nice-size kitchen there," Huey said.

"Is that alright? Isn't that trespassing?"

"I don't think it'll be a problem."

"Alright, then. What time should I arrive?"

Huey thought about what he had to do that day. "Is six o'clock alright with you?"

"That'll be fine. I'll see you at six, Huey."

"Goodbye, Sharon."

"Goodbye, Huey." He listened, waiting for her to hang up first before putting the handset back in the cradle.

Huey smiled. He <u>had</u> remembered the date and the phone call and the show. He just didn't want to sound too anxious to see her, not that his stumbling on the phone didn't give it away. Still, things worked out and he was going to be able to show off his cooking skills for her tonight. He had yet to decide what he would cook, but he had all day to come up with something. There were other pressing matters to attend to that were tugging on his brain. He had a truck that needed its original owner.

Huey got up from his desk and walked out the door, locking it behind him. Into the car again, it was time for a little road trip. He had another address on his sheet of paper to check out. This time, he had to travel several towns over. It was about forty miles through the countryside, but he didn't mind. Huey loved the scenery along the way. He had been this way many times. The town, Bethel Hill, was only a few miles away from his hometown, Mt. Clenney. As a matter of fact, he had to actually drive through Mt. Clenney to get to Bethel Hill.

He had been driving for about forty-five minutes with his arm out of the window and the music blaring on the radio before he entered Mt. Clenney. Looking at his watch, it was still early. He took his time driving around town. He passed his parents' old home, all of his old schools, and some of his old hangouts. As he made his way through his hometown, he started to feel a need to go somewhere he hadn't been in a while, and he decided that he had plenty of time to make that one stop. It was on the way anyway.

As Huey headed out of Mt. Clenney towards Bethel Hill, he pulled down this rarely-used gravel road just outside of town. As he traveled down the road, the trees and shrubs grew thicker and thicker. The road itself gradually turned from gravel to dirt and grass. The road became narrower and narrower, as the overgrown shrubs grazed the sides of the squad car. Once the road was completely dirt and grass, Huey stopped the car and got out. Overall, he had traveled about a half mile down this path. Stepping out into the grass, he looked out over an overgrown, but rather full cemetery.

Huey started walking in between vertical headstones and around in-ground ones. He was heading towards the center of the cemetery, knowing exactly where he was going. There were at least two hundred stones in this cemetery, not to mention the unmarked graves that were there. When he finally reached the center, he stopped in front of a large vertical headstone. Side by side, across the front of the stone, the words read Josiah Scott and Rachel Edwards Scott. Huey stared at the stone for a moment before speaking.

"Hey ma, pa. It's been a while since I've been out this way. I've been missing our little chats. I've been so busy with work lately, and usually by the time I'm done, it's too dark to come out here. The sheriff's been away for a week now, so I've been in charge. I think I've been handling it pretty well so far. I started seeing someone, ma. Tonight is our first date. Her name is Sharon Hunter, and she is a really sweet woman. Don't worry. I'll act like a gentleman. Just like you taught me. I'll keep you posted, too.

"Oh, and pa. I had to arrange a funeral for someone kind of close to you this week. It just happened to be... oh, I don't know... your brother! All these years, I've had 2 uncles, 2 aunts, and a cousin that I never knew. One family lived just outside the town I've been working in! However, don't be concerned. I'm not upset with you. Uncle Elias, the one I buried this week, left me a letter, explaining all that I needed to know. I understand why you did what you did and why you kept it a secret all these years. Uncle Elias even left me Ridgeway Farms and all his belongings. I am well taken care of now, so don't worry about me anymore. If I didn't mind disturbing you, I would have you, ma, Uncle Leroy, and his wife moved to the family cemetery. I don't think it would be a good idea, now that all of you have been gone for so long now. I will just have to keep coming back here to visit you. I don't mind, and I won't forget that you're here.

"I should probably get going now, though. I still have some police work to finish before my date tonight. She's going to come over, and I'll cook her one of your favorite recipes, ma. I miss you both greatly, and I'll come back soon, when I have more time. I love you both very much." Huey started to walk away, back to the car. He got five steps and stopped completely. He turned one hundred and eighty degrees and marched back to the headstone. He reached in his pocket and pulled something out, placing it gently on top of the stone. It was a small block of wood, whittled into the word <u>MORGAN</u>. Huey spoke again.

"I almost forgot. I wasn't too busy the other morning at the station, waiting for calls, and I whittled this for you. I thought you might like it. I've decided to

MORGAN
SCOTT

Josiah
1904-1975

Rachel
(nee) Edwards
1907-1979

"I drink," he said, "to the buried that
repose around us. And I to your long life."
—POE

change my last name back to Morgan and I think it's a fine time for you to do it, too."

Huey smiled, waved at the headstone, turned back towards the car, and walked away from his parents again. Getting back in the car, he drove in reverse the whole half of a mile back to the regular highway. Backing onto the highway, he returned to his original journey, heading into Bethel Hill.

CHAPTER 23

He knew the streets fairly well. He only lived a few miles away for most of his youth. He looked at the address on his motor vehicle sheet again. Huey didn't recognize the house number, but he did recognize the street name. He was able to navigate through town to the opposite end, where this particular street was located. Going slow down the street, he searched for the house number on front porches and mailboxes.

Nearing the end of the street, Huey was running out of houses, but he still hadn't quite reached the number. At the end of the road, there was no house, but a long driveway and a mailbox. The mailbox had the number he was looking for from his sheet! He turned down the driveway and followed it back behind a small grove of trees. As he traveled down the dirt path, the sound of large dogs barking grew louder. Finally, as he pulled around the trees, Huey saw a beaten-up single-wide trailer with some fenced-in pit-bulls behind it. He hoped that he had the right address, but his badge and his gun would help protect him, if it wasn't the right one.

"Gotta stay on your toes," Huey mumbled under his breath to himself. He pulled up next to an old pickup truck and parked defensively behind it on an angle. The dogs continued to bark and jump against the cage walls as he got out of his car and approached the door of the trailer. He didn't turn off the safety on his gun, but he did undo the snap securing it in his holster. He knocked on the door and stepped three feet back while he waited for someone to answer.

Then, a woman answered the door, dressed in nothing but a fuzzy robe, that she was just tying shut as the door, opened, and fuzzy slippers. She had a lit cigarette hanging from her lips, half was ash and half was filter. Her hair was tussled, and her cheeks were flush. "Yeah," she said. "What do you want?"

A voice from behind her, deep inside the trailer, hollered, "Who is it?"

The woman responded, yelling back over her shoulder, with the cigarette not moving, "It's the puh-leese!" Her drawl was very thick and slow.

A rolling stumbling got louder as it approached the door, as a shirtless man emerged behind the woman. He was pulling his jeans up and buttoning them, tripping over things in the trailer along the way. "Afternoon, officer," he said over the woman's shoulder, as he stood up straight behind her, placing his hand on her shoulder. "What do we owe the pleasure?"

Huey looked at both of them and replied, "I'm sorry if I'm interrupting something, but I'm looking for someone."

"The woman asked, "Who you lookin' fer?"

216

Huey handed the sheet of paper to the woman. "I'm looking for the gentleman listed on that piece of paper there. He was once registered to this address. Do you know who he is?"

"She looked at the name. "Sure, I do." She paused.

"Well?" Huey asked.

"That's my husband," she replied.

Huey pointed at the man behind her, "And I take it that he is not?"

"No, he is, too," she said.

Huey was confused.

"That man there... " she pointed at the paper. "...is my ex-husband." The man behind her butted in, "I'm her husband now. That man there was my ex-business partner."

"I see," said Huey.

"I left him over a year ago. We was separated for a while before that, but we was a-both still livin' here," she said.

"Is that when you stopped working with him, Mr... uh?"

"Maness. Mr. Alvin Maness," the man answered. "About eleven months ago, he decided that he couldn't stand seeing me with his wife anymore, so he ended our partnership together. She and I started seeing each other while they were separated."

"We're married now, though," she interrupted.

"And your name is?" Huey asked.

"Cora. Cora Maness. Are you from 'round here, sheriff? You don't look fer-miliar."

"Actually, I'm a deputy sheriff from Fellowship."

Mr. Maness asked, "You're an awful long way from home, aren't you deputy?"

"I'm originally from Mt. Clenney, but now I work and live in Fellowship."

Mrs. Maness asked, "Why all the questions about my ex-husband? Is he in some sort of trouble?"

Huey replied, "He appears to be missing. You wouldn't know where he is right now?"

"Not really," both the Manesses said in unison.

"You didn't kill him and sell his truck to an old man near Fellowship, did you?"

"Officer, I haven't seen that man since he moved out a year ago," she said.

Alvin responded, "I saw him a little over about three weeks ago. He was at the landscaping place a few towns over in Forrester Grove. He was stocking up his truck with some cinder-block. He saw me, but he never said a word. Guess he's still a little bitter over Cora and me gettin' married. That was the last time I saw him."

Huey was jotting down notes as they spoke. He mumbled to himself as he wrote, "So he was seen a little over three weeks ago <u>with</u> his truck. Now I have a truck, almost a month later, with no owner." He looked at Alvin. "What color was his truck when you saw it last?"

"White, I think. No, I'm pretty sure it was white," Alvin said. "Why? What color is it now?"

"Don't worry about it," Huey said.

"The truck used to have his name painted on the door with INDEPENDENT CONTRACTOR painted underneath it. That's what we did together. We were good, too."

"What do you do now?"

"You're lookin' at it. I haven't been able to find work in a while. He was the glue that held us together. But I do odd jobs to make money," Alvin said.

Huey looked at Cora. "Did he leave you, or did you leave him?"

Cora replied, "I told you. I left him. It wasn't over Alvin here, either."

"What do you mean? Why did you leave him?"

"I had been with him more than twenty years. He and Alvin only worked together maybe six or seven months. Anyway, over twenty years ago, while he and I were just newly married, I found out that he was cheatin' on me with some floozy. I believe that she was from that there town that yer from. He came back to me after I confronted him, but I don't think that he ever forgot her. We was already married, though. The morning I left him, he must have been dreaming of her, 'cause he called out her name in his sleep. I told him, 'Why don't you go find yer precious Junebug!' And that was the last thing I said to him. He said he wasn't going to live in this house anymore, but he did stay here for a few months. I never said another word to him. That's when Alvin and I started seeing each other. He took out most of his aggression with Alvin. He never said anything to me about it, though. I knew that he still loved me, but I knew that he would never let <u>her</u> go either. He moved out shortly after that. I don't know where he went, but I never saw him again. I was shocked that Alvin had seen him almost a month ago."

"So that's it, huh?" Huey asked.

"Yep," Cora said. "If you do find him, tell him that he's got a lot of stuff still here. He left with only a few pairs of overalls, some shirts, underwear, and socks. I feel bad that we still got all of his stuff."

"If I find him, I will tell him. Thank you for your time and cooperation." Huey re-snapped his gun holster. Alvin saw this and gulped. "Not a problem, sir. Thanks for stopping by."

Huey smiled, "I'll let you get back to whatever it was that you were doin'."

Cora looked kind of sad as she flicked her cigarette out of the trailer door. "Goodbye, officer." She closed the door behind her. The sound of the door closing started the dogs back up again. Huey could hear Alvin yelling out the back window at the dogs. "Will you shut up?!"

Huey got back in the squad car and pulled back down the long, dirt driveway. It was time now to go get ready for his date.

CHAPTER 24

As Huey drove back to Ridgeway Farm, he had about forty-five minutes to think. He tried to piece together what he had discovered over the last two days. Between Mrs. Glisson and the Manesses, he retrieved a lot of information. The truck owner was an independent contractor that originally lived in a trailer in Bethel Hill with his wife for a minimum of twenty years. In the beginning of his marriage with Cora, he cheated on her with someone referred to only by the nickname, Junebug. In the contractor's room at Mrs. Glisson's house, there was a sealed envelope addressed to the contractor signed by a Junebug, that appeared to be about twenty years old, based on the deterioration of the envelope. The contractor's affair occurred in Fellowship. About a year ago, the contractor left his already-failed marriage, his ex-wife, and his dissolved partnership with Alvin, and he moved to Fellowship, possibly in search of this elusive Junebug. He took only a few sets of clothes when he moved into Mrs. Glisson's house in Fellowship, mostly overalls for working. Working appeared to be the one thing to possibly take his mind off his troubles and his longings. The contractor had been helping Mrs. Glisson redo her house as rent payment. Mrs. Glisson mentioned the contractor working with a lot of cinderblock lately, and

Alvin noticed that he was loading up the back of his truck with cinderblock on the last day he saw him. The contractor's truck was white a month ago, and now it is blue. Somehow, Elias obtained possession of this man's truck. Elias lied about the previous owner of the truck on the day that Huey had pulled him over.

Huey was deep in thought when he realized that he was at the driveway for Ridgeway Farm. Time had flown so quickly, that he hadn't remembered driving all that way. He had to stop thinking about the contractor now. A lot of the pieces were fitting together, but now he had to concentrate on his date. Sharon would be arriving in an hour, and he was nowhere near ready. He pulled up to the barn, parked the car, and ran in the back door of the farm house.

Once he was in the kitchen, he stopped in his tracks. Huey had to decide what to do first. Should he start on supper, or should he take a shower and get dressed? Cooking the meal would definitely take longer, but if he got ready first, then he could still be cooking after she arrived. It would definitely turn out better with that scenario than if she had to wait while he showered and dressed himself. He could impress her with his cooking skills, too. His ma taught him well, and now he could show off for Sharon.

Huey ran up the stairs, taking two at a time, and he charged into the bedroom. Removing his uniform, he hopped in the shower and was back out in an instant. Taking a hanger of his clothes from Elias's closet that he hung there a few nights ago, he was dressed almost as quickly as his shower. He took a straight razor to his lathered chin and peeled off any five o'clock shadow. Nervous as he was, Huey almost slapped toothpaste on his face and aftershave on his toothbrush. A quick run-through of the comb through his still-wet hair, and he was physically ready. Mentally, he was still in the driveway.

Back down the stairs as fast as he went up, he was back in the kitchen. He grabbed Ellen's flowery, ruffled apron and flung it over his head, tying the straps behind his back. He rushed over to the potbelly stove and threw one fresh log inside. He grabbed some kindling that Elias had set alongside the stove, and he used it to light the wood inside the stove. While the stove was heating up, Huey grabbed a pot and filled it halfway with water from the sink. Elias might not have had natural gas piped in, but at least there was water from the well running into the house. He shucked some corn and threw it in the pot. Luckily, he had gone grocery shopping on the way home from Mrs. Glisson's house last night. He reached in his paper sack, pulled out three potatoes, and threw them in the pot with the corn. He put a lid on it and grabbed a skillet from the cabinet. Huey grabbed two thinly-cut steaks from the fridge and threw them into the skillet atop the stove. He still had twenty minutes before Sharon arrived.

After the pot had boiled the veggies for a few minutes, he lifted the lid, removed the potatoes, and returned the lid. Huey cut the potatoes into cubes and found Ellen's masher in a drawer. He pulled the almost-fully cooked steaks from the skillet and dipped them into a waiting egg-milk mixture, placing them on a plate. Removing a flaky pie crust from the paper sack, he crumbled that into a bowl, dropped each steak on both sides in the crumbs, and tossed cubes with some butter, salt and pepper, and he pulled the corn from the stove. Once the steaks were fully cooked, he removed the skillet, and he arranged everything nice on some china plates that Ellen had stored in another cabinet.

Huey had just finished setting the dining room table when there was a knock at the back door. He looked at his watch. It was six o'clock! He checked his hair in the hallway mirror and raced to the back door. His heart was racing from the anxiousness of getting supper done and tasting right; and his heart was pounding from the nervousness of showing Sharon a good time.

He opened the door for Sharon and held it open for her as she passed him into the kitchen. "Welcome to Huey's café," he said. She smelled really good and was dressed very nicely, too. Her strawberry blonde hair was down and wavy. He was used to seeing her at the diner with her hair up. This new look was definitely a good one. As she passed by him, she looked him up and down.

"Nice apron. Much different than that plain, old uniform," she said.

"Huh?" Huey looked down at the apron that he was still wearing! Quickly, he pulled the neck strap and untied the one behind his back. Huey tried to act fast and make light of his embarrassment. "What? This old thing?"

Sharon laughed, "That's alright. I have one just like it. I like it better on you."

Huey laughed. "Yeah, I do too." He winked at Sharon.

Sharon continued on into the kitchen. She looked around at the mess that Huey didn't have a chance to clean up. "Someone's been cooking in here. Smells good, too."

"Why, thank you," Huey said. "It's one of my mother's favorite recipes."

"What are we having?" Sharon asked.

"Let's go into the dining room, and I can show you. It's all ready to eat right now. I just finished a few minutes ago, so it's still nice and hot."

"Certainly," she said.

"After you, madam." He cradled his arms in the direction of the dining room.

"Such a gentleman," she smiled. She walked into the dining room to find a beautiful table setting. Huey had put out Elias and Ellen's finest silverware on a gracefully-elegant, lace table cloth. It was a long table, but Huey had placed the two place settings side by side to be closer to Sharon. The fresh cut flowers in the vase from this morning were in the center of the table. "It's quite beautiful," Sharon said.

"Let me," Huey said, as he pulled the chair out for her, and as she sat, pushed it back underneath her.

"I feel like a queen."

"You deserve to. You look like one," he said.

Sharon blushed and looked up at him. "Come, sit by me," she said. Huey hurried into the chair next to her.

"So, what are we having, master chef?"

"I cooked one of my favorite meals: Chicken-fried steak, corn on the cob, and mashed potatoes. I hope you like it."

"It looks delicious, Huey. I'm sure I will."

"I didn't have time to make a dessert. I'm sorry."

"After all this, I can't say I'd have room for it. This will all be just fine. You know, I'm so used to waiting on other people. It's so nice to be waited on for a change."

Huey smiled. "I'm more than happy to do it. I thought you might like this."

"Shall we eat?" she asked.

"Be my guest." Huey paused with his fork in his hand, watching as Sharon put her first forkful of chicken-fried steak in her mouth and chewed. "How is it?" he asked.

"It just melts in your mouth," she said. "We're not going to share this recipe with the diner folk. This will just be for us, ok?"

"Wow," Huey thought to himself. "That is the ultimate compliment from someone whose specialty is working with food for a living." He said aloud to her, "Thank you very much."

Throughout the rest of supper, there wasn't much conversation. The occasional, satisfying grunt from each of them broke the silence, but not for long. They both finished at roughly the same time, and Huey shot up from his chair to bring the dishes into the kitchen. As he reached for his plate, Sharon placed her hand on his waist. "Let me help you," she said.

"You are my guest, Sharon. I will not have you doing a job that you perform every day."

"This time, I don't mind... Really," she smiled up at him.

"I'm just going to bring the dishes into the kitchen for now. I'll do them later," Huey said.

"Nonsense, Huey. If you let me help you, we can get them done in no time. You cooked such a wonderful supper for the two of us that it's the least I can do. C'mon. I'll wash, you dry."

He looked into her eyes and saw that she was serious about helping. "Alright. Thank you."

"My pleasure," she said, as she grabbed some plates and led him into the kitchen. She put the plates in the sink, started the hot water, and put some soap in the mix. She looked at Huey as he stepped up next to her. She could see that he was a little upset about her having to do some work on their first date. She really didn't mind doing the dishes, though. Sharon felt as if she needed to make him forget about his concern. As she started washing the dishes, she nudged him with her elbow and looked him the eyes. "Do you want me to wait until you put your apron back on?" she giggled.

Huey snickered, "All the women in this town, and I pick a comedian." He bumped his hip sideways into hers. "Thanks," he said. "I mean it."

"I know," she said. "And you're welcome." As she continued washing dishes, Sharon started humming a tune that Huey was familiar with. He chimed in humming the song along with her. Soon, they had finished cleaning and putting away all the dishes. Once the last dish was back in its original spot, Huey looked at Sharon and asked, "Would you like some sun tea? I brewed some all day today."

"Sounds great."

"We can relax with a glass of tea and enjoy the show."

"Show? It's too late to go to the show now, Huey."

"Not this show. It's amazing, and we don't have to travel very far."

"Where is this show?"

"The living room."

Sharon looked at Huey with skepticism.

Huey said, "Trust me." He filled two glasses with tea, ice, and sugar. "After you, madam."

Sharon walked into the living room. Huey held a glass in the direction of the couch. She sat and took a glass from him. Huey walked over and turned off a lamp in the corner to make sure that there were no lights on in the room. The only light now was coming from the daylight through the picture window in front of them. He sat on the couch next to her.

"Now what?" she asked. "Where's this show?"

"Now we wait."

They sat there in silence for a few minutes until Sharon realized what Huey was talking about. It was the sunset. The most beautiful ball of red crept down from above the tree line towards the green earth below. It made the air around it a brush-stroked canvas of melted pinks, oranges, yellows, and purples. Sharon was in awe. She took a sip of her tea and laid her head on Huey's shoulder. It was quiet as the ball of fire dropped down below the horizon and the darkness set in.

Sharon looked up at Huey from his shoulder. "Ok. I get it now...And thank you."

"I told you," he said. "Let me go turn a light on. I'll come right back."

"You promise?"

"I promise, Sharon." Huey got up, turned on one light, and sat right back down. Sharon returned her head to his shoulder and wrapped her arm around his.

She said, "That is an amazing view. This house is aligned perfectly just for that."

"I can only imagine that Elias and Ellen sat here most nights and watched the same movie that we just saw."

"I know that I wouldn't tire of that." She paused for a moment before asking. "Speaking of Elias and Ellen, how is it ok that we are using this house for our first date? You never quite explained that to me."

"Well... that's because this house is mine now."

"Yours!" She sat up, lifting her head from his shoulder but still holding his arm. "But how?"

"Recently, I discovered that Elias Morgan was my uncle. He was my father's brother, and when he died, he left all that was his to me."

"Really?"

"I wouldn't joke about such a thing, Sharon."

"Wow." She got up from the couch, looking around. "All this is yours?"

"Yep. All of it...the house, the barn, the furnishings, the equipment, the vehicles, the land, the cemetery...all of it."

"That's incredible," she said. Sharon stood up and walked over to the bookcase. "Look at all these old books."

Huey stood up and joined her at the bookcase. He started pointing them out to her. "This one here is Ellen's old Bible. See how worn it is? You can tell it got used." He pointed to another one. "This is my grandmother's book of short stories by Edgar Allen Poe. My dad had one similar to this. He read it to me as a boy as she did to him." He grabbed yet another one off the shelf. "Oh, this book here is now very dear to me. Here, let me show you." Huey handed it to Sharon. "You can look at it, but please be very careful with it. It's quite old."

"What is it?" Sharon asked.

"It's the Ridgeway family Bible. It has the entire Ridgeway family genealogy handwritten in it, back to the ancestors from England."

"Wow!" she said.

"Exactly. That is why it is very dear to me," said Huey. He sat back down as Sharon gracefully turned the pages. Huey spoke again. "You know, it's great

232

now that I've inherited a family, a home, and all this stuff. However, there is one thing that still bothers me."

"What's that?" she said.

"There's this truck out in the barn... Well, it's a long story that you probably don't want to hear about on our first date." Huey thought for a moment. He wasn't so sure that he should be indulging all this information with Sharon. Technically, it's a police matter. On the other hand, he's known Sharon forever, and he trusts her completely.

"I don't mind really, Huey. I don't have to work tomorrow and I've got all night."

"Are you sure, Sharon?" Huey was still debating in his mind the ethics of whether he should cross that line and tell Sharon what's distracting him from their date.

"I'm absolutely certain." She reached out for Huey's hand. "If it's bothering you, then it's bothering me. And it's positively bothering our date. If it's something about work, I'll keep it quiet. Just get it off your mind, so we can get on with this date."

Huey sat down on the couch and looked into her eyes for a moment. He didn't know what it was inside that stare that proved to him that she was trustworthy, but it came over him in a rush. It may have been his fondness over her that pushed those normal distrusting feelings deep down, but he proceeded to tell Sharon about all that he's discovered over the last week.

"Alright. Here goes. Ever since I came to this town for work, I've had a friend in Elias. He's always treated me like a son. That is why I felt obligated to arrange his funeral. The day after his funeral, Hollis Woodward appeared as I was throwing the last bit of dirt on top of ol' Elias. He handed me two envelopes. One was Elias's will, leaving all this to me. The other was a sealed envelope with a letter from Elias, explaining why this estate was left to me. As I mentioned before, Elias is my paternal uncle. Shocked as I was by all of this, I started to go through some of Elias's things. In the barn, I came across this pickup truck. I had pulled Elias over on his way through town not more than three weeks ago. He explained that his brother had left him this truck when he died. Once I realized that his brother was my father and that my father never had a truck, I started snooping to get some answers. I called the state motor vehicle department with the VIN. They told me it was registered to someone else and it was a different color. Concerned even more, I went to the last known registered address, Mrs. Clara Glisson's house. You know Mrs. Glisson?"

Sharon nodded.

Huey continued, "Clara let me search the man's rented room. I found only a few overalls and a sealed letter, appearing to be about twenty years old and addressed to the truck owner. It was from someone only known as Junebug. Then, I went to the previous address of the truck owner. I found his ex-wife there, now married to his ex-business partner. They identified the truck and the owner. The business partner even mentioned seeing the truck owner a month ago, filling up his truck with cinder block. Mrs. Glisson confirmed that the man had a recent job working with cinder block. Now, we are current with everything, but I still have a lot of unanswered questions, and I seem to be at a brick wall. Can you conclude anything from what I just told you? I just need one clue, Sharon. One clue could get me moving again."

She asked, "What kind of questions do you still have? Let's start there."

"Well, let's see. Where is this missing truck owner? How did the truck change color in less than a month? How did Elias obtain the truck, and how is he involved in all of this? And finally, who is this Junebug?"

"Junebug, you say? That strikes a chord."

"Really?" Huey asked.

"Yep. Elias used to call his daughter, Sarah, Junebug all the time. It was his nickname for her. I don't know why though."

Huey grinned from ear to ear. "Sharon, can I see that book for a minute, please?"

"Sure." She handed over the Ridgeway family Bible to Huey.

Huey turned quickly to the pages within the book that had the genealogy listed. He searched for Elias's immediate family and there, right in front of his nose, was the answer. Just below Elias Jedidiah and Ellen Keathley Morgan was the clue to link Elias and the contractor: Sarah June Morgan. "Junebug," Huey said aloud. He looked over at Sharon. "I could... " Huey stood up, close to her, grabbed her cheeks with both of his hands, and kissed her full on the lips.

At first, she was shocked, but after realizing what just happened, she surrendered to his spontaneous advance. He let go of her face and stopped kissing her. He was shocked at what he had just done, too. He apologized. "I am sorry for doing that. I don't know what came over me. That is not how I usually handle things. I... I... "

"Huey, it's alright. I understand. I rather enjoyed it, but I understand." She smiled, blushing.

"Next time, I'll ask first."

"Next time? Does that mean you'd like to see me again, Huey?"

"I'd be a fool not to," he said.

"Well, sir, with that, I think I'll be going now."

"You don't have to leave so early, Sharon."

"I know, but I think you still have a lot on your mind, and I don't want to distract you."

Huey realized that without Sharon he would have still been stuck with no answers. Things were really starting to make sense now... because of her help. "Thank you so much for all your help, Sharon. You don't realize just how much you've done for me tonight."

"I think I do." She walked past him and winked, as she headed for the back door. Huey raced through the kitchen to hold the door open for her.

"I'll come by during the week to the diner to see you," he said.

"You do that." She walked past him out the back door. "Make sure you do that. Oh, and Huey... "

"Yes, ma'am?"

"You have a good night." She smiled and walked to her car. He walked half of the way with her but stopped at the edge of the house, never looking away from her. He stood there with his eyes following her the rest of the way there. Before sitting down in the now open car door, she waved at Huey. He waved at her, and then she got in, closed the door, started the car, and backed down the driveway onto the highway. Once she straightened out the car and her taillights disappeared behind the trees, he walked back into the house, closed the back screen door behind him, and went back into the living room. He looked down at the Ridgeway Bible, spread open on the couch. "Right there in front of my face. All this time." What a wonderful night Huey just had: for his investigation and for his love life.

CHAPTER 25

Sunday morning came, and Huey awoke with a smile on his face. He got ready and had breakfast with every intention of driving over to Sharon's place and surprising her with an escort to church. He left through the back door and headed to the squad car. Just as he put the key in the door lock, he stopped. He looked at the car and thought to himself, "Maybe Sharon wouldn't want to ride to church in the sheriff's car. That would just draw attention to us immediately." He didn't want to make her feel uneasy or uncomfortable this early in the relationship. It was too early to just throw themselves out there in front of everyone. Granted, just by showing up together, people would already start to gossip and mumble to each other, but Huey wanted to be subtle about things for Sharon's sake. He didn't know exactly how she was feeling at this moment in their budding courtship.

Huey had a problem though. His everyday car was parked back at the station. Even if he left now to switch cars around, he wouldn't have enough time to pick up Sharon and make it to church on time. Walking in late would draw the same amount of attention as appearing in the squad car. He still had to surprise Sharon, too. He wanted to give her a few minutes to soak that in and let her decide if she was ready to make an entrance together. What should he do? He was running out of time. "Think... Think, Huey," he said aloud to himself.

Huey looked up from the car and happened to glance over at the barn. He saw the lock on the door and walked over to it. Unlocking the door and opening it, he stood there as the light entering the barn revealed what could be the solution to his problem: the truck. The truck, though newly painted, was still very low-key. It wasn't flashy or loud. It was just a truck. No one would surely notice it pulling into the church parking lot. It would probably put Sharon at ease, knowing that she could slip into church without causing a scene. There were problems, though. Huey had a moral and ethical dilemma spinning around his head. Although Elias had left him everything in the will, there was no proof that Elias ever owned this truck. Elias had lied to Huey about his brother giving him the truck. Huey's father never owned a truck, and Elias's other brother, Leroy died before this truck was ever manufactured. The previous owner was still missing and Huey was still investigating the case on a personal level.

Huey put his hand on the door handle of the truck, but he stopped at that point. He couldn't really take this truck without feeling horrible about it during _and_ afterwards. Besides, after what he told Sharon last night about this truck, he was sure that she wouldn't get in the truck anyway. It was getting too late to show up at church, and Sharon didn't know anything about Huey escorting her to church. He may as well give up on his good intentions for now.

Huey took his hand off the door handle. He circled the truck, looking at it from every angle. Then, he stopped. Out of the corner of his eye, he noticed a shiny reflection coming from the opposite corner of the barn. Tilting his head back and forth as he slowly approached it; Huey could not decipher exactly what it was, even after he stood directly in front of it. Whatever it was, it had been poorly disguised under a white tarp and some hay. If Elias had hidden it there, then he must have done it in a hurry.

Moving the hay aside, Huey lifted the tarp that had barely been strewn over the top of this shiny object. He stepped back two feet to take in what he had uncovered. It was a professional paint sprayer and a few cans of dark blue spray paint. The color matched the finish of the truck. Now, the puzzle was filling in its own pieces and things started making sense.

Elias had been the one who painted the truck. He did a good job, too. Why did he paint the truck, though? Was it because he didn't like the color, it needed a paint job, or was he trying to cover something up? He thought he knew Elias pretty well, but then again, Elias kept the whole family secret from him for at least fifteen years. What could Elias possibly be hiding about this truck? It was never reported stolen, but the previous owner appears to be missing, too. If the owner went missing around the same time as the truck, then it couldn't have been reported as stolen.

Huey walked back over to the truck and opened the passenger side door. He opened the glove compartment. It was empty. No vehicle registration... No insurance cards... Nothing. Elias was thorough. He checked underneath the seats... nothing. He pulled the seats forward... still nothing. Finally, he pulled down the visor on the driver's side and something fell. Huey walked around to the driver's side and opened the door.

He picked up the object and stared at it. It was a picture of a woman. The picture was old, at least twenty years or so.

Who was this woman? Could this be the mysterious "Junebug?" Huey, with Sharon's help, had discovered that "Junebug" was Sarah. Sarah was Elias's daughter, but she also appeared to be the love interest of this missing contractor. So, who put this picture here? Was it Elias, or was it the contractor?

Huey stood back up, out of the truck, and he closed the driver's side door. He leaned back against the cinderblock wall, staring at the picture. And then, it came. It was an incredibly pungent smell that crept up his nose and set up shop there. It was horrible and eye-watering. He didn't know why he hadn't smelled it before. Maybe it was because he hadn't stood in that specific area of the barn until now? He thought back to Thursday. Maybe this is what Hollis smelled that day? Hollis had been standing right here. Well, it certainly wasn't a manure smell like he had told Hollis. But, where was it coming from? Huey walked back and forth, sniffing along the wall. In every direction, the horrible scent got fainter and fainter, so Huey traveled back to his original spot where the odor was strong and irritating. It appeared to be coming from behind the cinder block wall. A dead animal, perhaps?

Huey looked to his left. A sturdy ladder was propped up against the wall. How convenient? He made sure that the ladder had a solid footing for support and then placed both hands on the ladder. Looking upward towards his destination, he spotted a broken beam with a short, frayed rope dangling from it. "Huh," he said. "Didn't notice that before."

As he made his ascent up the ladder, Huey noticed the stench magnify in strength. What was behind this wall that smelled so bad? Once he reached the summit of this fortified barrier, he paused to brace himself and prepared to stomach whatever was causing this putrid stink. He slowly shifted his head and neck sideways over the side of the wall, peering down into the gap. "Coon or fox…whatever it was, it's dead," he mumbled to himself. The first eye to drift over the edge spotted the source, and Huey quickly snapped his head and neck back over to the original side of the wall from where he came. As a natural instinct, he clutched his hand over his mouth and nose as a precautionary measure to prevent himself from losing the breakfast he had slaved over this morning.

Huey proceeded to look back over the wall. There, in an advanced form of decay, lay the body of a man. Flies amassed the exposed body parts and circled above him as well. The extreme summer heat had ravaged this poor man's body. His face was no longer recognizable. Who was this man behind the wall? How was Huey supposed to identify him? He looked down again, still covering his mouth and nose. All he could see from his position was a man, possibly around fifty years old with what appeared to be jet black hair and overalls. He was slumped over on his side and covered in concrete dust. Huey started back... wait a minute... overalls?

Then, it came to Huey. All the thoughts from this week dropped on his shoulders and took his breath away. The puzzle was complete. Huey knew who this man was. "How could I be such a simpleton?!" he shouted out loud. It was obvious that this was the contractor and missing truck owner that Huey had been searching for these last four days. Dead would explain missing. This guy had a closetful of the same overalls back at Clara Glisson's house. He must have been hired by Elias to work on this wall. There are tools, materials, and freshly-opened empty bags of concrete scattered all over this barn. Was this an accident, though? No, I don't think so," Huey mumbled to himself.

From all of his discoveries, Huey had several valid conclusions backed up by evidence. Finding a letter from Elias's little "Junebug" to this contractor confirms that the two had some sort of relationship together. Sarah, according to the family Bible and tombstone out back, died just over twenty years ago, which is approximately how old that letter was. Elias hired this guy, probably knowing exactly who he was. Maybe Elias felt as if this contractor was partially responsible for Sarah's death? "I don't know how Sarah died, but to do so at thirty years of age usually isn't natural. It was probably either murder or suicide..." Huey thought. "...Especially if Elias would go to all this trouble."

Huey looked further down into this tomb. The light peering through the wall cracks highlighted two things that he hadn't initially noticed. There appeared to be a picture lying there on the ground next to the contractor's body, and there seemed to be a message painted on the inside of this cinder block wall. It had to be fresh because the wall is new. Swatting away the flies, Huey lowered his torso down the inside of the wall to read the message, careful not to tumble into the depth. Trying to decipher the words while suspended upside-down, he read slowly, but clearly. "I want you to remember... before you are forgotten." Oh, yeah... Definitely not an accident. He could only assume that the picture next to the body was, without question, a photograph of Sarah.

The timeline matches up. The contractor was last seen about a month ago, confirmed by the ex-business partner and Mrs. Glisson. Considering the heat, it is possible that this body has been lying here, exposed to the air and other elements, for at least three weeks to a month.

Huey pulled himself back up to the ladder and stepped down to the safe side of the wall. He turned to face the truck. "Now we have this truck," he muttered. Obviously, by discovering the paint equipment and now the body, Elias painted the truck to cover up the murder. Then, he lied to Huey about obtaining it, possibly to protect him from the repercussions of eventually discovering his relationship to him. Plus, it was a nice shade of dark blue.

CHAPTER 26

Huey thought back to Thursday, when he finished covering Elias with dirt. Just before he was startled by the appearance of Hollis Woodward, he was examining the blade of the shovel that he used to bury Elias. It had two small, dark-red spots on the blade. He had forgotten about that because of Hollis and he didn't think of it as a crucial detail for any reason. It was, back then, just an odd happenstance. Where was that shovel anyway? Hollis was helping to carry the tools back that day. Where did he put it? Huey scanned the barn and found it lying by the back wall atop some fairly new two-by-fours. He grabbed it and brought it outside the barn, into the sunshine. Lifting the blade up to his face, he spotted the two infinitesimal stains. Now that he could examine them closer and now that he knew what had happened, Huey could easily determine that those were definitely blood stains. Knowing that Elias's strength at his age probably didn't kill the contractor with this blow, but it sure persuaded him behind the wall. This shovel was definitely evidence in the crime. And Huey had used it to bury the criminal.

He stood there, thinking back to the other book on Elias's bookshelf that was lacking dust, the collection of short stories by Edgar Allen Poe. He thought back to his childhood and Elias's childhood. Both he and Elias were prepared for this story. It had been read to them both at least a hundred times by Huey's father and Elias's mother. They could both recite it verbatim from memory. "Of course," Huey said. "The Cask of Amontillado."

Huey marched back into the barn with the shovel. He gave the entire barn a once over. Elias had been prepared to cover his tracks, but he never quite got the chance. Huey stood there looking at the remainder of materials Elias had left in plain sight that were inconspicuous until now. There was a bottle of bleach sitting right by the foot of the ladder, obviously to cover up the smell. Elias never got to do that. If he had, then it may have been awhile before the contractor was discovered. Who uses bleach in a barn anyways? There wasn't a lot of mortar mixing or cinder block left to build anymore walls. Elias was probably going to just seal off the top of the wall.

Huey had to handle all this evidence carefully. The sheriff would start back again tomorrow. He couldn't mess this up. There was a lot of detail to explain and a lot of evidence to tie things together. Huey had a lot of work in front of him to deal with. He stood there holding the shovel in his hand, thinking about how Elias stood here, holding this same shovel not long ago.

"Poor Elias," he said. Sure, it was definitely a bad thing that Elias killed this man, but Elias had his reason. Now that Huey knew the full story of his family's troubles throughout the years, he pitied Elias for all that he encountered. Elias had achieved what he had set out to do, but now it was all going to be unearthed. It was going to tarnish the name that Huey had so boasted about no more than four days ago. People wouldn't remember the words Huey had said anymore. And if they did, it would just be to mock him. The townsfolk in Fellowship were relentless with their gossip. That is what kept Elias from returning to church.

He was embarrassed and now Huey would be, too. Huey had recently bragged about returning to his original family name. That would just be thrown back in his face as an insult now. People would only remember Elias for this grisly murder. And they would hold that against Huey, too. He could just hear it now, "You're the nephew of that murderer, aren't you?" The legend would carry on for generations even after he died. This is a small town, after all. Word travels fast, and stories tend to stick around in the minds of these close-knit townsfolk. Things were definitely going to blow up starting tomorrow.

Huey could fix this though. He could make things right. At least for him anyway. He grabbed the bottle of bleach and shovel, and he ascended the ladder. He threw the shovel over the wall, down by the body. He opened the bottle of bleach and emptied it directly onto the contractor's body. Every last drop. He tapped the bottom of the plastic jug to make sure. It did help the smell, but now bleach fumes filled the surrounding air. He climbed back down and ran over to the paint sprayer.

Huey loaded up all the equipment and extra cans of paint and threw them over the wall. He pulled the picture out of his shirt pocket that he found in the truck, ripped it to shreds and threw that over too. He picked up anything that he thought could ever be tied to the contractor, even if it wasn't, and he dropped it down by the body.

Huey looked back by those two-by-fours from earlier. He rustled them together and carried them up the ladder. Placing all but one atop the wall, he used the one piece on his hand to measure the gap between the barn wall and the cinder block wall. The plank was a quarter inch longer than the gap. They were all cut to the same size. That's what these were for. Elias had them pre-cut ahead of time, and the contractor never noticed them. These were to support the cinder block that would seal off the top of the wall. Not condoning what Elias had done, Huey smiled at the intelligence of this man. He was impressed by the detailed planning Elias had done to accomplish such a feat and get away with it.

Jumping down off the ladder, he grabbed a hammer and was back up at the top again in the same amount of time it took him to get down. Carefully spacing each plank, he tapped them all in with the hammer, so that each cinder block he placed would sit flush with the top of the wall. One by one, he brought each cinder block up the ladder and placed each on top of the wall for the time being. He hopped down off the ladder and ripped open the only remaining bag of mortar mix. He tossed the empty bag over the wall, too.

Then, like a man possessed, Huey raced over to the house to turn on the hose by the spigot. Then, he raced back to the barn. Even though church was still in session and hardly anyone ever came this way anyway, Huey couldn't take any chances of anyone seeing him do what he was doing. He grabbed the hose end and watered the mix. He ran to the house one more time and back to shut off the water. Then, grabbing a bucket, he used the trowel sitting there to scoop mortar into it. He carried it up the ladder and set it on the wall.

Now, he had to act quickly. Coating each side of each brick, he laid them all into place on top of the framed structure that he just erected. He laid them all on their side so that there were no exposed holes atop the wall. They fit like a dream. Elias had calculated perfectly and there were no bricks remaining on the ground.

Before Huey placed the last brick in its final resting place and smoothed the top over with a layer of mortar, he looked down into the now-darkened tomb. He took one last look over the rotting corpse below. He pitied the contractor. Obviously, he had wronged Elias and Sarah, but was this the price he had to pay? Certainly, God would have judged him accordingly. Elias took advantage of a weakness that he saw almost immediately in the contractor: pride in his work. He made the assumption that the contractor would take his time and do a good job...and he was right. Elias just had to wait until the right opportunity to execute his plan. If the contractor had done a subpar job, he may have been able to escape the two-foot wide prison, but this time, pride would be his downfall.

Huey looked down and did the only thing he could think to do. He stopped and prayed. He prayed for forgiveness and salvation for the contractor, Elias and himself, too. He confessed the sins of all three of them and asked for peace for Ellen and Sarah. He prayed for his parents and anyone else that had been hurt, unbeknownst to them. He knew that God already was aware of all that had transpired here, but Huey didn't feel whole until he had come clean about it all.

After the prayer, Huey spoke down into the chasm below, cupping his hands around his mouth and with a resounding, dramatic voice, yet still hoping that no one would hear him. "The amontillado, Fortunato! The amontillado!" he shouted. And after a brief pause, he whispered, "P.S. Mrs. Glisson misses you." He spread the mortar on the final block and placed it in its awaiting spot. Then, he coated the top with a layer of mortar and smoothed it out. He inspected his work and got down from the ladder. As he cleaned off the tools, he was saddened by what he had just done, but he couldn't help feeling a little bit of pride in his work. "Not bad for a sheriff's deputy," he said. Realizing what he just said, he stopped smiling and locked the barn behind him as he exited. He went into the house to clean himself up, and to absorb all that had just happened. Huey remained in the house for the rest of that Sunday. The sheriff would be back tomorrow, and he wanted to prepare himself for the Monday ahead.

CHAPTER 27

Monday morning arrived too quickly for Huey. He didn't feel prepared to go into work this morning. Sheriff Holmes would be back from his week-long vacation. Huey was exhausted from his ordeal yesterday, both physically and mentally, and it showed this morning. He got ready really slow. He took his time getting in the shower and dressing. He was trying to prepare himself with answers to any questions that the sheriff might have. That way, he wouldn't get caught up.

Once he had his breakfast and had no excuse to prolong going into the station any longer, Huey left the farmhouse and headed for his squad car. He still had plenty of time before he was scheduled to come in, but he was never much later than this on a regular day. He didn't want to appear as if it was anything but a normal morning. He arrived with ten minutes to spare and didn't dawdle any longer in his car. "Just go in and get it over with," he said to himself. The sheriff didn't have that keen of an eye to notice that Huey was acting slightly different than normal. As long as Huey played it cool, things could go on as if nothing ever happened yesterday. "Well, no more stalling." Huey got out of the car, stretched his arms out, and then proceeded inside the station. He stopped inside the door and looked around. There was no sight of the sheriff, though his car was parked outside. He walked towards his desk to sit down and check his workload for the day. He pulled back the chair and stepped one foot forward to sit.

"Morning, deputy!"

The words shot through the air, loud but deep. It shocked Huey into standing rigid with one hand still on the chair. Huey shivered and rolled his eyes before turning to greet the man behind the voice. As he turned, he cracked his best fake-smile to make the sheriff feel welcome. Huey had enjoyed his time without the sheriff. He was able to think for himself and answer to no one. People treated him with more respect while the sheriff was away. Now, it would return to Huey having to stand behind the man on all the calls.

"Good morning, sheriff. How was your vacation?"

"Fine. Just fine. It's good to be back though."

"Did you go or do anything special?" Huey asked.

"I went to visit my brother's family in Kentucky. Once I got there, I didn't do much of anything. We just sat around and talked most of the time."

"Sounds relaxing."

"It was. It definitely was. I'm all rested up now to get back to work."

Huey half-smiled at him, "Great."

"Well, did anything new or exciting happen around here while I was gone? It feels like I've been gone forever," the sheriff said.

"Here?" Huey paused, thinking about all that had transpired over the last week. "No, nothing exciting, really." He paused again, pretending to think back. "Oh... you remember Elias Morgan?"

"That ol' son-of-a-gun. 'Course I do. What's ol' Elias been up to?"

"Not much of anything lately," Huey said. "He died last Monday."

"No kidding?" The sheriff was shocked. "What from?"

"Heart attack. It appeared to have happened quickly. He didn't look as if he suffered at all."

"Wow," the sheriff muttered. "Guess he's up there with Ellen."

"Hopefully," Huey mumbled.

"You know, Elias is only a few years older than me," said Sheriff Holmes. "Soon, that could be me. I'd better start thinking of a replacement for when that time comes. Know anybody, Huey?" Huey sat in the chair, not saying a word. It was quiet for a moment.

"Hey… you could be my replacement, couldn't you, Huey? You can handle this, right?"

"Been doing it for a week now," Huey mumbled again.

"What was that, Huey? Did you say something?" the sheriff asked.

"I was just saying that those are big shoes to fill, but I would be honored to try."

"Sounds good. Gotta be elected in though. Think you can do it?" The sheriff chuckled at Huey.

Huey kept his mouth shut. No sense in stirring up trouble.

"That reminds me, Huey," Sheriff Holmes said. "Do you know Mrs. Clara Glisson?"

Huey's ears perked up.

"I got this call here at the station just before you walked in."

Huey was nervous. "Was the call <u>from</u> her or <u>about</u> her?"

"It was about her. Pastor Jones called me this morning. He says that she must have died sometime during the night. He found her this morning while paying a social visit to her."

"Pastor Jones found her?" Huey asked aloud.

"Yes, sir," the sheriff replied. "Is there something strange about that?"

"What?" Huey's thoughts were racing through his head.

"I said... Is there anything strange about that?"

"What?" Huey said again, this time calmer to deflect suspicion.

"Pastor Jones finding Clara Glisson dead."

Huey stumbled to cover his thoughts. "Oh... no. I was just thrown a little bit finding out about Mrs. Glisson. She seemed fine... "

"Seemed fine?" the sheriff interrupted. "Have you seen her lately?"

"Yes, sir."

"When was that?"

Huey slowly muttered, "On Friday. I paid a visit to her home."

"Was it a personal visit or police business?"

"Well... she called about her lost cat, so I went over to help her," Huey said.

"Huey?"

"Yes, sir?"

"I've known Clara for thirty years. She doesn't own a cat."

Huey paused for a brief second, and then replied. "Yes, sir, I know. Clearly the years haven't been good to her memory. I went over there to clear things up."

"Well, that was awful nice of you, Huey. It's a shame that she didn't hang on much longer. At least the last person that she probably saw did something considerate for her. You know, Huey, that I was just going to head on over there, but since you were so thoughtful to her, why don't you go in my stead?"

Huey breathed a sigh of relief. He had avoided questions about both deaths from this last week and was able to get away from the sheriff for a little while. He got up from his desk and looked at the sheriff. "I'm on my way over there now." He grabbed his hat and keys and walked over to the front door, opening it. He placed one foot out the door when the sheriff spoke again.

"You know what they say, Huey? They say that deaths come in threes... "

Huey stopped in mid-stride.

"...Hopefully, we won't get one more."

Huey thought about the contractor behind the wall, before turning to respond to the sheriff. "I don't think that'll be happening in this town, sheriff. Besides, that's all superstition anyways. You don't believe in that kind of stuff, do you sir?"

The sheriff paused, "Well... no, but it is sort of weird that we've had two deaths in the same week. People seem to live forever in this town. Heck, maybe I'll be sheriff for another twenty years."

"Maybe this town needs a third one," Huey whispered.

"What was that?" the sheriff asked.

"Nothing... nothing, sir."

"Huey, either I need a set of hearing aids, or you need to speak up. I saw your lips move, but I couldn't hear you. If you ever want to fill my shoes, then you need to use your voice. You can't expect to earn people's respect until you learn to convey your authority."

Huey replied, "Yes, sir."

"I'm sorry, son. Whatcha say?"

"Yes, sir!!" Huey snapped back as he slammed the door behind him. He got in the car and headed over to Clara Glisson's house.

CHAPTER 28

On the way over to Clara Glisson's house, Huey thought about how he had just been there. He couldn't imagine that, even in her advanced age, she was that close to passing. She seemed physically healthy. Absent-minded, but well. And that was on Friday. Three days ago. What happened?

Huey had a short drive from the station to Clara's house. As he pulled in the driveway, he noticed a familiar car parked across the street. He parked his car near the rear of the house and walked around to the front. Climbing the steps, Huey opened the door and walked right in.

From the corner of the living room, a voice spoke out. "Doesn't anyone knock anymore?"

Huey wasn't startled. He knew who was there already. "Pastor Jones, I see you're still here."

"I told the sheriff that I would stay until someone else got here. I didn't want to leave Mrs. Glisson alone. I expected the sheriff to show up, not you deputy. Oh well, I guess I can go now." Pastor Jones rose from his chair in the corner and proceeded to the door.

Huey stepped halfway in front of Pastor Jones's path and gently placed his hand on the pastor's chest to stop him. "If you don't mind...I'd like to ask you a few questions before you leave."

"Huey. Now that you're here, I have preparations to make for Mrs. Glisson's funeral arrangements. I really must leave."

"Pastor. You were the first one on the scene where there was a death involved. You are the best judge of what happened, and I need some clarity. Now...will you please sit back down and help me fill my notebook?"

The pastor stepped backwards, away from Huey's still-outstretched hand and sat back down. "Alright, Huey," he said.

"Deputy Morgan."

"Right, right. Deputy Morgan," the pastor muttered. He paused for a moment in confusion. "I thought it was Huey Scott?"

Huey's chest puffed out slightly in pride. "It was, Pastor Jones. I have just recently uncovered the revelation that I am, in fact, the nephew of Mr. Elias Morgan, and that my father's original last name was Morgan, so out of respect, I am gracefully returning to what should have been. It's not legal, yet, but it soon will be."

"Really," the pastor had an intriguing look on his face. "All this time... and you never knew? What are the chances?"

"Enough about me though. That's not relevant." Huey felt that the pastor was already digressing the

263

conversation. "At what time, Pastor, did you arrive here at Mrs. Clara Glisson's home this morning?" Huey opened his notebook as he spoke. Pen in hand, he awaited the response from Pastor Jones.

"I suppose it was around eight-ish or nine-ish."

Huey looked up from his pad. "Ish? You are the most punctual person I know, Pastor. 'Ish' is not in your vocabulary. What time did you get here?"

"Eight o'seven."

"That's better," Huey smiled. "And did you have an appointment with Mrs. Glisson?"

"No, I did not, Hu... Deputy Morgan. Every couple of weeks, I pay a visit to my parishioners that are shut-ins. It helps me to keep in touch with the community, and it helps them feel right spiritually. I just picked Clara randomly."

"Did you knock before entering the home?"

"Of course, I did. I don't have the authority that a fine officer like you has to enter the sanctity of another's home without their permission. That would be awful rude of me." The pastor gave Huey an upsetting look.

"I see," Huey snapped back. "Was there an answer?"

"No. There was not."

"Did you knock a second time before entering the premises? Clara, I mean, Mrs. Glisson is... was hard of hearing."

"Yes, I did. There was still no answer, but I knew that she was home. She's always home."

Huey jotted more information down on his notepad. "She could have been asleep."

"That was unlikely. She was just like me, an early riser. She would get cleaned up, eat something, watch the morning news, and then, it was time for her... "

"...Stories. Yes, I know. Trust me, I know."

The pastor smiled.

"So, Pastor, you found her dead?"

"Yes, sir."

"Where is she now?"

"In her bed. She's exactly how I found her, lying on her back in her very own bed."

"Did you touch anything?"

"No, sir. My fingerprints are all over this house, though. I'm her pastor. I visit a lot."

Huey wrote that information down. "Is there any reason that you might believe Clara Glisson died from anything besides old age?"

"No, Officer. Why? What are you implying?" The pastor had an unsettled look on his face.

"I'm not implying anything. I'm asking routine questions that my job requires me to ask." Huey stared hard at the pastor for a full minute or two. "I guess that's enough questions... for now. I need to examine the scene and report back to the sheriff. You can leave to make Mrs. Glisson's arrangements."

"If you need me for anything, Deputy... "

" ...I know where you work."

"Right," Pastor Jones said. He stood back up from his chair and walked past Huey. Huey didn't budge from his spot, and the pastor had to step around him to leave. The pastor, perturbed from being interrogated, shut the door hard behind him and walked over to his car. Huey heard the engine start, and the car pull away from its spot across the street.

Once he was certain that the pastor was long gone, he went in to observe the body of Mrs. Glisson. It appeared that she hadn't even gotten out of bed. She must have died in her sleep. Still in her night gown and slippers, she looked so peaceful. Lying on her back with her arms crossed over her chest, Clara was clutching a book. Huey approached Mrs. Glisson and, without touching her, pivoted his head to see what she had been reading.

It was the Bible. Of course, it was. Pastor Jones was here. Mrs. Glisson was not the type of person that read the Bible every day. She didn't even appear to read it when clergymen were near. Not to say that she wasn't a believer, but she definitely wasn't a reader.

266

Pastor Jones must have had something to do with this. "I'll have to ask him when I see him again."

Nothing else appeared to be out of order. Huey would have to let the coroner decide the vital facts about Mrs. Glisson.

Just then, a thought appeared to Huey. Looking around the house brought up thoughts about his visit last week to this home, which dug up thoughts about the contractor. All of the contractor's stuff was still here in the back room, including that letter. Huey had expunged all remnants of the contractor... except for his personal belongings. Surely when someone cleans out this house, they will come across his clothes and that letter. This was the final opportunity for Huey to eradicate all traces of the contractor, once and for all.

Huey ran to the back porch and found an empty box. He raced into the contractor's bedroom, placed the box on the bed, and started going through dresser drawers. They were all empty. The only items in the room were those overalls in the closet. Cora Maness wasn't kidding. Huey grabbed all the pants from the hangers and folded them. He stacked them in the box, grabbed the hat box <u>and</u> the letter.

Huey remembered from the first visit that the top two dresser drawers had stuff in it, though. There were other clothes and gas receipts. He grabbed the box and left the room. Over in the room where Clara did her own laundry were the missing clothes. They were folded and stacked, ready to be returned to the dresser drawers. Clara must have been washing and re-washing them with the hopes that it would help return her tenant to her.

In the kitchen, near the back porch, sat the trash can. Huey peered down into it and found the missing gas receipts. Clara must have figured that he didn't need those anymore. Huey reached down and plucked them from the can. All of it went into Huey's box. When he was quite certain that he had it all, he proceeded out the back door and over to his car. It was convenient that he had parked so close to the back. He approached the trunk and while supporting the box with one hand, removed his keys from his pocket with the other hand. He used the keys to pop open the trunk lid, and shifted some things in the trunk while still holding the box to make room for it.

As he placed the box in the trunk, a voice startled him from behind. "What have you got there, Deputy Morgan?"

Huey didn't even have to turn around to see who it was. He recognized the voice immediately. He had just heard it no more than twenty minutes ago. "Pastor Jones," he said while turning to greet his uninvited guest. "How can I help you?"

"I was on my way back to the church, and I remembered something that I was going to mention to you. I did a U-turn and came right back before I forgot it. I didn't expect you to be out of the house already."

Huey was curious. "That was courteous of you to return so quickly. What did you recall?"

Pastor Jones stood there for a moment, silently. "Now I forget... I'm sorry. I'm usually pretty bad when it comes to remembering things, so I try to take care of them immediately. Now I've just wasted both of our times."

In an agitated voice, Huey responded. "That's alright. If you remember later, then you can contact me at the sheriff's office. As for now, I have to return to work, and I need to finish up here, so if you'll please excuse me?" Huey began turning back to the trunk.

"What do you have there, officer? I hope that you don't mind me asking?"

"Actually... " Huey thought that he had skirted the issue of the contents of the box, but obviously he hadn't. He scrambled for an intelligent response that would throw the pastor for a loop. " ...now that Mrs. Glisson is no longer with us, any and all possessions of hers are under police scrutiny before being released to her next of kin... which I do believe is not you. As a leader of this community, however, I do not feel that there is any harm in divulging that in this box is... "

The pastor's ears perked up with meddlesomeness. "Yes?"

"Donations."

The pastor's chest sunk a little in disappointment. "Donations?"

"Yes. Before Mrs. Glisson passed, I had spoken with her last week. She still had a lot of her deceased husband's old clothes, and she thought that they might be of use to someone else, instead of collecting dust and taking up space in her home. She asked me if I could assist her in distributing them to the proper individuals in need. I told her that I knew just the people to handle such a thing."

Pastor Jones stepped in to reach for the box. "Why, thank you, Huey. The church is always willing to lend a hel... "

Huey stopped him, mid-sentence, extending his arm in the path of the pastor. "Thank you, pastor, but the church has done a lot already for this community. It's about time that the community helps itself... Besides, give credit where credit is due. Sometimes, the congregation is under the impression that you undertake more responsibility than you can handle... And we both know that isn't exactly true. Right, Pastor?"

"Are you truly insulting a man of His Word right now? Do you realize what you are saying?"

Huey smiled. "I know that you realize what I am saying. His Word hasn't really flowed from your lips in a long time. You can speak fluently enough to confuse the masses, but you can't speak truthfully. You've been reading from the Bible, but it's the Pastor Jones Edition."

Shocked by Huey's statement, Pastor Jones turned and huffed in animosity as he stormed down the driveway without saying another word.

"Situation averted," Huey said, breathing a sigh of relief. He removed the gas receipts and letter from the box before closing the trunk. He placed it into his pockets, got in his car, and left for the office to finish his work day.

CHAPTER 29

Although it was only a short distance back to the office, Huey took his time driving back there. He was startled by Pastor Jones as he packed his trunk, and he needed to calm down. He made a few circles around the town square, looking in on the diner to get a glimpse of Sharon working inside. She noticed as he paused one last time, and she waved at him with a beaming smile. This instantly settled his mind, and he completely forgot about the incident outside of Clara Glisson's home. Huey felt like it was time to go back to the office now. He pulled into the parking lot and went inside the sheriff's station. Sheriff Holmes was still there, sitting at his desk on the phone. Once he saw Huey enter, he finished his phone call and hung up.

"Didn't think you were coming back, Huey."

Huey walked over to the sheriff's desk.

"What took you so long?"

Huey was surprised by the questions the sheriff was asking. He knew why Huey was going to Mrs. Glisson's home. He knew that it wasn't an easy task to investigate a death. Why would he be so concerned about how much time Huey spent on the call?

"I was performing a routine investigation of Mrs. Glisson's case. Is there a problem with how long I spent there, sheriff?" Huey's response had a minute hint of

272

anger in it. He was upset that Sheriff Holmes was questioning his authority, judgment, and investigation skills.

The sheriff was amazed at Huey's defensive tone when speaking to his superior. "Huey, son, I don't appreciate the tone of voice that you're opting to use right now."

"Well, sir, I guess that I don't appreciate the insinuations that you're making right now."

The sheriff sat back in his old, wooden chair that creaked loudly as it leaned back. "And what exactly do you believe that I'm implying, Deputy?"

"From the tone in your voice, sir, it sounds as if you think I'm lacking the intelligence or speed to conduct a proper study of the case that I was given. You've known me for how long now, Sheriff? Am I really like that?"

"Huey, Huey, Huey. You're making a big something out of absolutely nothing. I was just joking with you, except for the statement where I didn't think you were coming back tonight. You've been working really hard lately, Huey, especially in my absence. I assumed that you'd just head straight home after your search of Clara's house. I know how precise you get when you're working. I never doubt your judgment or skills for a second. Why do you think that I felt so comfortable leaving on vacation for so long a period of time. I trust you, Huey... and I would never hesitate leaving this community and its citizens in your capable hands at any given time. You know that, right?"

Huey was stunned. Sheriff Holmes had never opened up like that to him. He never truly knew how much respect the sheriff had for him. Huey had mixed emotions right now, demonstrated by the half-smile, half-frown on his face. The sheriff knew it, too. Huey was happy about the trust he felt now, but was embarrassed and disappointed in himself for the way he had just acted. "I'm so sorry, sir, for raising my voice to you and accusing you of not believing in me. I've never truly understood what your opinion was of me until now. It was just a long wait for the coroner after I had finished, and then, there was P... "

"Pastor Jones, right?" the sheriff interrupted.

"Yeah. How did you know that Pastor Jones was there?"

"He made the initial call to the station about Clara, remember? He was going to wait until someone from the sheriff's department showed up. He was there when you arrived, right?"

Huey was totally confused now. There were so many excuses that it was getting hard for him to determine between the truth and his cover stories. "Oh, right. I thought that you meant when he came ba--."

Huey stopped in mid-thought, trying to avoid putting his foot in his mouth, but it was too late.

"He left and came back? Interesting." The sheriff was intrigued. He pulled a small, black book from his desk drawer and started jotting down some notes.

Huey leaned slightly towards the desk to glance at what the sheriff was writing. The sheriff looked up from his book at Huey.

"What's that, Sheriff?" Huey asked.

"Oh, this?" Sheriff Holmes held up the book rather quickly. "Sometimes when I get thoughts in my head, I like to jot down notes in here. It helps me to clear my mind, knowing that even if I forget something, it should already be written in this book. I can rest easy then."

"Oh," Huey said. "That's a good idea... Did you just write something from our conversation?"

The sheriff paused for a moment. "No, no. I just remembered something from earlier and didn't want to forget it again." He put the book away in his desk. "You were saying that Pastor Jones came back to Clara Glisson's house?"

"Yeah, he did," Huey said.

"What did he want?"

"He said that by the time he had returned, he had forgotten what he was going to say to me."

"That's strange," Sheriff Holmes said. "He had plenty to say to me, and he remembered it all."

Huey got even more nervous. "He was here? When? What did he say?"

The sheriff chuckled, "He was here no more than an hour ago. He said that he had just come from Clara's house, and how disappointed he was that I wasn't the officer to arrive on the scene. I explained to him that I had a lot to catch up on and that you were more than capable to handle such duties. Then, he proceeded to inform me that you were just a 'rookie,' and that I would have been better sending my dog in your place."

The expression on Huey's face dramatically changed. His eyebrows steeply slanted towards his nose. His forehead creased like yardage on a football field. His nose scrunched upwards, as his jowls drooped to the floor. His cheeks tightened as his entire complexion turned a shade of fire engine red. The volume of his voice increased and the pitch dropped as he growled out a response to what the sheriff had just told him. "He said what?!"

"Calm down now, Deputy," the sheriff said, sternly. "I straightened him out. I told him that you are the best deputy I've ever had, and there was no better man to investigate anything in this town. I told him that if he couldn't keep his opinions under wraps and keep his mouth shut, then he was no longer welcome in our station. And when he started to get defensive, I told him to shut his mouth and listen for once. This isn't

Sunday, and I don't need a sermon, especially from him."

Huey calmed down and laughed a little. "What did he say to that, Sheriff?"

"He said that I had some audacity to speak that way to him. He told me that he was a man of the church, and that alone should demand my respect."

Huey laughed again.

"You notice, Huey, that he didn't say that he was a man of God. He said that he was a man of the church. I pointed that out to him and said that a real man of God wouldn't speak that way about others. He wouldn't harbor feelings like that inside, either."

"How did he take that criticism?" Huey asked.

"He just kept getting more and more angry. I just kept pushing all the right buttons. He never stopped talking, either. I thought his head was going to explode. He started spewing off scripture, stuttering and stumbling along the way. Now, Huey, I'm not much of a Bible reader, but I know that he was making some of that stuff up. And when he was finally reaching his boiling point, I called him a liar, told him to shut up, and held the door for him to get out. He stormed out, vowing never to come back in here again. I yelled back at him that his vows meant nothing to me. He screamed like a little girl, got in his car, and sped out of here."

By now, Huey was in uncontrollable hysterics. Somehow, he managed to stop his laughter and wipe the tears of joy from his face. "Sheriff, thank you. It has been a long week since you were gone. I had to deal with some unfamiliar situations and some unsavory people. I persevered, but I am exhausted. That little story about the pastor just made my day. Heck, it made my week. I appreciate you backing me up when I'm not around. That makes me feel as if I actually mean something to someone and that my job matters."

The sheriff smiled. "Huey, your job does matter. If it wasn't for you, why, I couldn't go on vacation." He laughed. "You do look tired, and you did a fine job while I was gone. Now it's time for you to take off. Starting now, Huey."

Huey was surprised. "But Sheriff... what about Mrs. Glisson? I was in the middle of... "

The sheriff interrupted again. "Not your problem. Leave me your notes. Pastor Jones and I will take care of her arrangements. I don't want to see you in that uniform for a week, Huey. You understand me? You rest up. You need it."

"But Sheriff... "

"Go on now. Remember, a week."

Huey's thoughts quickly drifted to the contractor's stuff from Clara Glisson's home. Huey had taken it all, so there was nothing left for the sheriff to find. A week off would give him ample opportunity to dispose of the items properly and discreetly. Huey smiled at the thought and nodded at the sheriff in gratitude.

"Thank you, sir. I shall utilize the time well to catch up on rest. I appreciate it."

"The town of Fellowship appreciates you, Deputy Morgan."

Huey started his way out of the station, but stopped at the door, looking back at Sheriff Holmes. He thought to himself, "I never got the chance to tell him that I'm related to Elias... Did he just call me, Morgan?"

CHAPTER 30

Huey waited a second until he was certain that Sheriff Holmes was done speaking, and then he walked out the door of the station and got in his car. He sat there for a moment. He took a deep breath... and cleared his mind. What was he going to do first? He closed his eyes and waited to see what image his mind would come up with.

It was almost instantaneous... Sharon. There was no second guessing it. His subconscious wouldn't lie to him. If he wasn't working, or dealing with cleaning up after Uncle Elias, then his desire was to spend time with Sharon. And he hoped that she felt the same way, too.

He saw the look on her face as he circled the diner today in his squad car. She was glowing. Before another thought could cross his mind, he started up the car and put it into drive. He almost drove through a red light, but Riley Austin had been driving through the green, going the opposite direction, and he laid on the horn to stop Huey from proceeding. Riley shouted some obscenities while shaking his fist at Huey, but Huey just smiled and waved back. Old man Riley just got angrier and sped up faster after the intersection. Huey continued on to the diner, once Riley had passed.

Huey pulled up to the diner and parked the car. He peered into the elongated windows from within the car.

He spotted a glimpse of her, but she didn't notice him. He emerged from his seat and closed the door behind him. Huey entered through the door, and the little bell attached to the door rang out. Sharon didn't notice it, though. She was busy delivering orders to the cook.

Huey attempted to sneak in behind her.

"Afternoon, Hu... " a patron spoke out.

Huey shushed him and pointed at Sharon. The patron understood and nodded back at Huey. Huey snuck up to the bar and sat down on a stool just behind Sharon.

He shouted out, "Man, this service is terrible! What's someone got to do around here to get an egg salad sandwich? I mean how hard is that? You don't have to cook anything!"

Sharon was startled and turned around to defend herself. "Listen, sir. I've been working my tail... " She looked down at her assaulter to find him smiling back at her. "Huey!" Her grin went from ear to ear, as she removed her apron and smacked him with it.

"Hi," he said.

She blushed and shyly responded, "Hi."

The cook behind her rang his bell, letting her know that an order was ready. "Order up." The bell woke her from her trance.

"What are you doing here?" she asked. "Are you off-duty? Are you hungry? Would you like something to eat?"

Huey laughed at her obvious nervousness. "Yes, yes, and... yes," he responded. Sharon smiled at him, realizing how transparent she was to him. "The sheriff realized how hard I've been working and how exhausted I am, and he rewarded me with a week off. I just got off now, and you were the first thing I thought about."

Sharon giggled with embarrassment. "That is awful sweet of you, Huey. You know how much I miss you when we're both working."

"Yeah, and I was thinking... "

"Hold that thought, Huey. I have to deliver this food. I'll be right back." Sharon turned, grabbed the plates, balanced them on her arms, and scurried out into the dining room area. Two minutes later, she returned behind the counter, empty-handed. "I'm sorry, Huey. What were you saying now?"

"What I was saying was... "

Ding. The order bell rang again. "Order up."

"Remember what you were going to say. I shall return." Sharon scooted off with another array of plates and returned with some empty glasses.

"Not bad. Six-dollar tip," she mumbled to herself. She looked at Huey.

"I'm sorry. Go ahead, Huey."

"I guess I just wanted to... "

"Did you want an egg-salad sandwich? I'll make one for you, if you'd like?"

"Thanks," Huey said. "That'll be great."

Sharon hustled over to the refrigerator and removed the already prepared egg-salad from it. She removed some bread from the loaf behind the counter and proceeded to make the sandwich. She returned to Huey's presence and slid the plate on the bar in front of him.

Huey grabbed her wrist, gently to get her attention. She was still holding his plate. "Sharon."

She was startled, and she stopped moving to stare at him. "Yes, Huey?"

"I just wanted to know if you'd like to come over this evening. I miss you, and I'd like to see you."

Sharon smiled at him, realizing that she had been rushing around him this entire time. Quietly she said, "Yes, Huey. I would love that."

The order bell rang again. "Order up." Sharon didn't move. She was still staring at Huey as he continued to hold her wrist. The bell rang again. "Order up." Still, no movement. The cook rang the ball hard this time. "Sharon!"

"Huh?" In confusion, she turned to the cook. Huey was still holding her wrist.

"Order up." The cook was perturbed, but she didn't care.

"Right," she said. Sharon turned back to Huey and whispered, "I have to get back to work now."

Huey removed his gentle grip from her wrist. "OK. Sorry. I'll go now." He picked up the sandwich from the plate. "I'll take this with me. How much do I owe you?"

Sharon smiled. "It's on me. I got a six-dollar tip, remember?"

Huey smiled back at her as he got up from his stool. "Thank you. Just come over whenever you're ready. I'll be home the rest of the day."

"I'll see you later." Her eyes followed him to the door.

He walked backwards up to and out of the door, never losing sight of her. She waved at him slightly as he stepped outside. He waved back as the door closed in front of him. He kept looking in the window and smiling, as he got in his car and pulled away for home.

CHAPTER 31

Huey left the diner feeling good. Although he never thought about it before, it was about time he got to spend a week off of work. He had earned it. And now, he could finally spend some quality time with Sharon. He drove back to Ridgeway Farm with a smile on his face. He backed his car down the driveway and parked it by the barn door.

Huey had to hurry if he wanted to get everything done that he had to before Sharon arrived. He emerged from the car and slammed the door shut. Running around to the rear of the car, he used his key to pop the trunk. He turned to the barn door, unlocked and opened it, then pivoted back. Giving a quick look around, he reached into the trunk and wrapped his arms around the box of the contractor's stuff. Jerking back, Huey propped the box onto the trunk ledge to get another grip in a better position around it. He quickly spun around and placed it just inside the barn door on the floor, before closing the door and re-locking it. Slamming the trunk shut, he went in the farmhouse back door to get some stuff done in the house.

He straightened up some couch cushions, a stack of papers on the kitchen table, and his pile of shoes and boots by the back door. There were still dishes in the sink from the night before and that morning, so Huey plugged the sink, put some soap in it, and started the hot water running.

The water was so hot that Huey was surprised he still had fingerprints after a few dishes. He scrubbed each of the old dishes quickly and set them gently in the drying rack. Some of the dishes were cracked and chipped. Some were broken and had been glued back together. Huey was trying to preserve this home and everything in it, so he was trying to be gentle. He was in a hurry, though. He didn't know when Sharon was going to arrive, and he still had that box sitting inside the barn door.

He finished the last dish and drained the sink. He rushed up the stairs and removed his uniform, draping it across a chair in the corner of the bedroom. He stepped into the tub and turned on the shower. The water was freezing. Huey had used all the hot water to wash the dishes. Huey hurried through the shower to get out and warm up. He dried himself and scrounged through his clothes for something to throw on temporarily until he was done with his chores. He found a comfortable t-shirt and a nice pair of jeans and got dressed.

The only real chore remaining that Huey <u>had</u> to do was to get rid of that box in the barn with the contractor's stuff inside. By now, the sun had almost completely set below the horizon. He raced out the back door of the farmhouse and over to the barn. Keying the padlock and flinging the heavy, wooden beam away, Huey swung the door open. His eyes scoured the barn for something to help get rid of the evidence. He locked onto a 55-gallon drum with the lid removed. Elias had been using it to hold rusty tractor parts, but it was only half full.

Huey shot over to it but couldn't lift it, not full anyway. He braced his right foot behind him, and then, with his torso as close to the drum as possible, he leaned into it and tipped the drum to its side and down to the barn floor. Some, but not all, of the tractor pieces shot out of the drum opening and across the barn. Huey looked into the barrel to see how much was left. He grabbed the closed end of the drum with both hands. Squatting with his knees completely bent and his center of gravity up against the drum lid, he rose to a fully-erect position, dumping the remainder of the contents onto the pile before him.

The drum was now completely empty and easily manageable. Huey tilted the barrel onto its lip edge and rolled it out the door of the barn, around the corner of the building and stopped next to the tool shed. He laid it on its side and then raised it back up, so now, the opening was again back on top. He was out of breath from all this lifting and spinning, but he couldn't stop now. Sharon would be here soon.

He raced back inside the barn, just inside the door. He squatted again, grabbed the corners of the heavy box, and grunted as he stood up with the last remaining articles of the contractor in his hands. He was tired now, and his knees slightly buckled as he walked out the barn door. He made it in one trip, though. Propping the box on the edge of the barrel, Huey opened the cardboard container and began removing each piece individually. Inspecting each one carefully, as any good deputy would, he tossed them, one by one, into the drum.

Huey looked down into the almost empty box. There was one item left: the letter. He reached down and picked it up. Holding onto it tightly with both hands, he could feel his family connection, flowing through his veins. The event that occurred shortly after the writing of this letter affected his family so much. Huey's first cousin wrote only one other letter after this before taking her own life. It's almost as if this was the "cause letter" and the other was the "effect letter."

Sarah June Morgan was his first cousin and his only cousin. He never got the chance to meet her, and this letter would be his only chance of getting to know how she truly felt inside. It was still sealed.

Huey was at the fork in the road, but he didn't have time to be there. He had to destroy the evidence now, but could he let go of that letter? One side of the coin said that it was evidence that could bring a lot of shame and sadness to the Morgan family. On the other hand, he would be losing a piece of his family by destroying it. There were so many different ways to handle this. He could open it, read it, and keep it hidden. He could open it, read it, and burn it. He could leave it sealed, out of respect for Sarah, but hold onto it. Finally, he could leave it sealed and burn it to dispose of it properly.

Huey kept leaning in so many directions that he couldn't decide. He shoved the letter in his back pocket for now, and he grabbed a log with some kindling from the woodpile by the shed. He stood, hovering above the drum to get one last look inside. Then, he slammed the log down into the barrel, mashing down the pile of items. He walked over, grabbed a second log, and plunged it in before gently placing the kindling in random spots. Ducking in and out of the barn, he hooked a can of gasoline from the floor by the tractor. He also picked up a book of matches from a coffee can sitting on top of Elias's workbench.

Huey opened the cap of the gas can and vented it from the opposite side. He poured the contents into the drum, generously soaking everything. He set down the gas can and reached into his front jeans pocket for the book of matches.

There was only one left in the book. He had to make this one count right now. He thought for a moment, and an idea came to him. He started ripping the empty box into pieces, and he threw them into the barrel. Huey saved one last piece of cardboard, and he removed the match from the book. Striking the match, he lit the cardboard in his hand and used that piece to ignite everything else in the drum. It was a success! He threw the dwindling piece of box in his hand into the now-growing, but contained blaze.

It was now completely dark outside, especially way out in the country where he was. Huey stood in front of the glowing drum, staring directly into it. It was the only light source for at least a couple of miles. He had forgotten to turn on lights in the house before racing out of it. Smoke rose from the drum and dried out Huey's eyes. Even in the late summer heat, the nights would cool off slightly, and this new source of warmth was welcomed by Huey. He remained there, holding his palms towards the flames.

This fire before him stirred up deep emotions inside. It was a cleansing flame. It brought a lot of the bad times in the Morgan family together and eradicated them in one shot. It returned the status of the Morgan name back to a level of honor. Huey's shoulders dropped in relief as the weight of guilt was released by the smoke and the crackling of now-forgettable memories in front of him. He would have teared up, if not for the smoke refusing to allow him to physically do it. Instead, he smiled. He stood there, continuing to stare and smile into the distinct, nose-burning smell of a gasoline-started fire.

Huey stared into that drum, deep in thought and oblivious to anything surrounding him. Without a sound of someone approaching him from behind, a voice spoke up, playful and gentle.

"Why, Huey Morgan, what is it that you're doing back here?"

Huey never heard it.

"Huey Morgan... I've got to get used to calling him that... Huey Morgan, do you hear me?"

The barn, the shed, the trees, the fire... They all absorbed the voice. Alas, Huey still blanked it out. It was Sharon, and she was slightly frustrated. "Huey, you invited me over and you're just going to ignore me!" she shouted.

Finally, her rant broke through Huey's concentration and startled him. He spun around to greet her.

"Sharon. I'm sorry. I didn't hear you come up. I was entranced by the fire."

"Obviously."

"How long have you been here?" he asked, nervous and embarrassed.

"I just arrived. I was going to knock on the back door, but I saw the glow and you standing back here."

She looked past him to the drum. "Burning anything special?"

"Huh?" He looked at where she was focused. "Oh, no. Not really."

"You're getting rid of evidence, aren't you?" She looked at him, slyly.

Huey was startled. "I'm sorry, what?!"

"Relax, Huey," she smiled. "I was just joking."

"Oh, right. I just didn't expect that from you." He sighed slightly.

"Seriously. What's the fire for?"

Huey thought, quickly. "I thought it might be nice for us to sit out tonight with a fire after supper. By the time we're done eating, it should have died down to a glowing pile of ash. Sound nice?"

Sharon smiled. "Sounds wonderful."

"I still have to cook though," Huey said.

"I'll help you. We'll make something quick and easy."

"I'd like that. Let's go inside."

Sharon turned back towards the house. Huey caught up to her and placed his hand across her back to help guide her back to the house.

CHAPTER 32

The next morning, Huey woke with the sun beaming in on his face. He had forgotten to pull the shade down last night and now, he was suffering for it. He sat up and pivoted, so his legs were dangling from the side of the bed. He sat there with his head slouching and his palms propping him up. Lifting one hand, Huey rubbed his eyes and then held his forehead. Still groggy, he looked down at himself. He must have slept in his clothes from yesterday, as they were still on. Not really sure about what happened last night, he tried to focus on remembering some details.

And then, a noise came from behind him. It was a muffled, stretching sound, and Huey spun around in the bed to see where it was coming from.

There, lying on the bed next to him, was Sharon. She, like Huey, was fully clothed in the previous night's fashion. They had both been lying on top of the comforter on the bed. The sound from Huey spinning in the bed woke Sharon. She slowly opened her eyes to see Huey's smiling face staring back. Now, Huey remembered what happened.

Sharon sat straight up in confusion. Huey saw how tense and apprehensive she was, so he extended his hand to caress her face. "Relax," he said. "It's o.k."

"But... but... " she stuttered.

"Nothing happened here last night. It's all right."

"You don't understand," she said.

"I understand that we had a nice time last night. We had a nice supper. We sat out by the fire. We had some nice wine. Thank you, by the way. You fell asleep out there, and I carried you up to this bed. I was tired too, and I conked out right next to you. So, why are you so tense?"

"I'm supposed to open the diner this morning, Huey. That's why. I know that nothing happened, but I wouldn't be ashamed if something did. I like you, Huey. I like you a lot."

Huey blushed. "I'm sorry. I didn't know that you had to work today. If you'd like to shower here, then I can drive you in to town?"

Sharon smiled. "I'd like that, but what about my car?"

Huey responded. "I'm off for a week. I've got nothing to do. I can pick you up, and we can have supper again tonight. How's that sound?"

"Huey Morgan, you are just an incredible man. You have yet to say or do anything that would keep me away from you."

"Can I get you some breakfast while you're in the shower?"

"I hate to ask, but if you could just brew some... "

"...coffee?" Huey blurted out. "Consider it done."

Sharon slid over in the bed and gave Huey a kiss on the cheek. "I have a spare set of clothes in my car if I ever get stranded somewhere. I can change into those."

She shuffled off the end of the bed and stood up. She ran out of the room, down the stairs and out the back door. Huey heard the screen door slam as the spring retracted. He peeked through the curtains and down to the driveway as Sharon skipped to her car like a little schoolgirl. She opened the trunk, removed the clothes, and slammed the trunk shut. Then, she skipped back to the back door as Huey peered on. The screen door slammed again, and the footsteps stomped louder as she neared the top of the stairs.

Sharon poked her head back in the open door frame and stared at Huey. "You sure this is all right?"

Huey laughed. "Go now, before you're even later for work. People are starving outside your diner right now."

"Most of them just want a cup of coffee... and they don't even tip. They can wait for me to shower."

"You tell 'em, Sharon," Huey smiled.

She laughed as she turned and backed out of the open door. She found the bathroom, turned on the light, and shut the door behind her. Huey stood in the hallway until the bathroom door was closed, and then he went down the stairs and into the kitchen. He grabbed the coffee pot and began filling it with water from the kitchen tap. He continued to smile with thoughts of Sharon as he filled the percolator with coffee grounds.

Suddenly, there was a knock on the back screen door. Huey was startled enough to drop the lid of the coffee can in the sink. "Who could that be?" he said.

He left everything as is and walked to the back screen door. Opening it, he saw a short man dressed in a black suit. Huey thought to himself, "Awful hot to be wearing a suit."

Huey addressed the stranger, "Can I help you?"

"I'm looking for an Elias Morgan. Is Mr. Morgan at home?" the man asked.

"No, sir. Mr. Morgan is not home right now."

"Might you have any idea when he will return?"

Huey was curious about all the questions about Elias. "I guess that all depends on what this refers to."

"Well, sir, it has come to my office's attention that Elias Jedidiah Morgan may have passed on. I was sent out here to verify this. Can you tell me if this is true?"

"What exactly is it that your office concerns?"

"My name is Elbert London, and I work for the Tennessee State Highway Commission."

Huey understood. "I did notice the government plates on your car."

"Good. Now that you know I work for the government, can you please answer my question? Can you please tell me if Elias Morgan is still alive?"

"No, sir."

"No, you can't tell me, you won't tell me, or he's not alive."

"The latter."

Elbert London grew a smile on his face, as he thought to himself, "That stubborn old man is finally gone!" He looked directly at Huey. "Well, sir, if that is the case, then do you reside here?"

"Yes, Mr. London. I live here."

"Did you purchase this land from Mr. Morgan?'

"No, sir."

"May I speak with the current landowner, then?"

"Yes, sir."

There was a long pause. Elbert was waiting for an additional comment from Huey. Elbert spoke: "Well? Is he home?"

"Yes, sir."

Huey was getting a kick out of all this. He was making Mr. London antsy, and he saw how upset he was getting.

"Can I speak with him?"

Huey continued, "Go ahead and talk. I'm listening.'

Elbert was completely confused now. "I thought that you said that you didn't purchase this land from Mr. Morgan?"

"Yes, sir. I didn't."

"But you're the landowner?"

"Yes, sir."

Elbert stared down at his clipboard in utter bewilderment. He flipped through the paperwork, skimming each page. "According to my records, Elias Jedidiah Morgan had no living descendants or listed heirs. Might I inquire as to how you obtained the property?"

"Let's start over, Mr. London. Your paperwork is wrong. I am not a direct descendant, but I am related and a rightful heir. Let me introduce myself. My name is Huey Scott Morgan, and Elias Jedidiah Morgan was my uncle. At least six months before he died, Elias arranged a last will and testament, and I was named as the sole heir of his entire estate; not that it is any of your business."

"So you're the man I need to talk to?" Elbert interrupted.

"No, I'm the last person you want to talk to. I understand now why you're here, Mr. London... and I think that you need to leave my property."

"But, Mr. Morgan, my office has been attempting to obtain a small portion of this land for over twenty years now. This location is perfect for an interstate that would save this commun... "

"Allow me to do a favor for you, sir." Huey interrupted.

"Are you going to let the state obtain some land for development?"

"No, sir. I'm going to save you some time. I'm going to let you walk away from here, knowing that you, or anyone else from your office, will never have to waste your time coming back here ever again."

"Mr. Morgan, I think that you don't fully understand what my office can and will do with or without your cooperation."

"I don't think you fully understand what I can do to you or anyone else from your office, if you continue this barrage of harassment."

"Is that a threat, Mr. Morgan?"

"No, sir. That is my solemn and final vow. Is that understood?"

"Yes, sir."

"I just want to say that I believe you're ignoring an opportunity to... "

"...keep this land in my family for the next two hundred years. I'm not ignoring it. I'm embracing it. Just as Elias Morgan would have wanted me to do. This is bigger than just me and you. This was bigger than Elias. He knew it and now I see it."

"I can see that we are never going to get anywhere now. We were just waiting for Elias to pass to get another shot at seizing the land that we need to make our road. I guess that I'm going to have to convince my office to try another option."

"Your office could have saved more than twenty years, if it had just taken Elias's first 'no' seriously."

"I guess. They'll just have to propose another route" said Elbert.

"The government is just stubborn, and they don't take the word 'no' very well. They don't seem to be very intelligent, either" said Huey.

"How's that?"

"Well, they don't appear to be able to read... especially the sign on the front door."

Elbert chuckled. "Funny... Your uncle said the same thing."

Elbert turned, wiped his sweaty brow, got into his government-issued vehicle, and backed out of the driveway without saying another word to Huey. As he pulled away from the farm, Sharon came downstairs from the shower. She was fully dressed in her waitress uniform, but her hair was still soaking wet and pulled back into a ponytail. She looked at Huey.

"I heard voices," she said. "Were you talking to someone?"

"No one important," Huey replied as he handed Sharon her fresh brewed coffee. "The Morgans won't ever hear from them again... C'mon... " He looked at Sharon. "...let's get you to work."

82714717R00173

Made in the USA
Lexington, KY
05 March 2018